WAS IT MURDER?

Sloan was thinking about Bill Fent. "Let's get this quite straight, sir. He died from injuries received in a road traffic accident . . ."

"Agreed," said Superintendent Leeyes.

"What we are checking on is whether someone tried to kill him first. Which makes it attempted murder."

"Agreed," said the superintendent. "Or murder full stop. If he had the accident because of the poison."

"The lawyers are going to like this one, sir, aren't they?"

"Never mind about the lawyers," grumbled Leeyes. "What about us?"

"I couldn't agree more," said Sloan fervently. "Give me a straightforward manual strangulation any day of the week. At least you do know where you are then . . ."

Bantam Books by Catherine Aird
Ask your bookseller for the books you have missed

Slight Mourning

Catherine Aird

BANTAM BOOKS

TORONTO • NEW YORK • LONDON • SYDNEY • AUCKLAND

SLIGHT MOURNING

A Bantam Book / published by arrangement with Doubleday & Company, Inc.

PRINTING HISTORY

Doubleday edition published August 1976

Bantam edition / February 1982
2nd printing . November 1982
3rd printing . December 1983
4th printing . November 1984
5th printing . . . . . May 1986

ISBN 0-553-25631-9

Bantam Books are published by Bantam Books, Inc. Its trademark, consisting of the words "Bantam Books" and the portrayal of a rooster, is Registered in U.S. Patent and Trademark Office and in other countries. Marca Registrada. Bantam Books, Inc., 666 Fifth Avenue, New York, New York 10103.

PRINTED IN THE UNITED STATES OF AMERICA

H   14 13 12 11 10 9 8 7 6 5

*For Margaret Shorthouse (but for whom, etc.)
with love.*

"Slight mourning will be worn
 during the visit . . ."

Postscript to a letter written by
an equerry in 1889 inviting a guest
to Sandringham House for the weekend.

ONE

Miss Cynthia Paterson considered herself something of a *connaisseuse* of a good funeral.

This had been born of long practice. She was the only child of a country rector and attendance at village funerals large and small had been part of her lot in life for as long as she could remember.

She was at one now, sitting in her usual pew in the great empty church of St. Leonard in the parish of Constance Parva in the county of Calleshire. High above her, in the church tower (late Norman, with Victorian embellishments), the funeral bell tolled at regular intervals. That was the tenor bell (cast in 1622), which was her favourite.

It had the words "Alfred bade me be wrought" inscribed on the metal, and when she was small—she'd been a ringer ever since she had been strong enough to handle a rope—she used to wonder who Alfred had been. There was something else carved on the bell too: something which she had never forgotten, although it was a good many years now since she'd been right up to the top of the bell tower.

> I to the Church the Living call
> Too the grave do summons al.

In those days, of course, bell-ringing had been important. They'd rung the death knell when anyone in the parish died, accompanied by the "tellers" which gave the age and sex of whoever had passed away. There was nothing like that these days. Ringing wasn't what it had been when she was young—and that wasn't yesterday, either, as

Cynthia herself would have been the first to admit. They didn't even always have the funeral bell at a funeral any more now.

This funeral was different, of course.

Gregory Fitch would have stopped whatever he was doing up at the timber yard half an hour ago. Then he'd have come down to the church and taken off his jacket in the same purposeful manner as he did everything else in life. She could visualize him now as clearly as if she'd been standing in the bell tower beside him: a sturdy countryman, with muscles thickened by the saw and the axe, to whom bell-ringing was effortless.

He'd have one eye on the clock, that was certain. A minute bell was a minute bell when Greg Fitch rang it. There was something else that was certain too, and that was that there would always be a funeral bell when one of the Fent family was buried.

Miss Cynthia Paterson turned her attention back to the church. She wasn't the only one sitting there even though she had been early. Being early for church was something else born of long experience. It had been one of the few things her father had insisted on, and old habits die hard. For forty years he had ministered to the parish of Constance Parva and read and re-read his books—and got to the church in good time.

She aligned her hassock with a deft hook of her right foot. Perhaps if her mother had lived he would have taken preferment when the opportunity came his way—but her mother hadn't lived and her father had stayed on at the rectory of Constance Parva while Cynthia herself had grown up and passed almost without noticing it into middle age. At the same time, with her father, middle age had slipped equally imperceptibly into old age and a Christian life had ended with a Christian death.

Which was more than could be said for him whom they had come to bury today. A Christian life, perhaps, but nobody could call it a Christian death. That didn't mean that the Book of Common Prayer didn't provide for it. The Prayer Book provided for almost everything you could think of—most of it in the Litany. If she closed her eyes now she could conjure up a vision of her old father intoning, "From lightning and tempest; from plague, pestilence, and famine; from battle and murder, and from sudden death . . ."

She didn't mind being early. It was pleasantly cool in the church even though the hot summer sun was shining outside. The stained-glass windows on the south side of the church glowed warmly, splashing their colours all over the chancel. It was August. August, which the ancients called the death month, though she didn't know why. She would have to look it up. She still had all her father's books.

Her own much-thumbed, most-used book—her gardening text-book—decreed that in August the gardener could go on holiday with no worries provided that he has "mown the lawn, watered thoroughly, and asked a friend to pick the fruit and vegetables." Cynthia Paterson couldn't afford holidays but she did ease up a little from the professional gardening she did the rest of the year round.

Her various employers up and down the village didn't seem to mind. She had noticed before now that they themselves had slackened their interest in their own gardens by the middle of August—except those with the church flowers on their minds. They remained perpetually anxious; but not the others. April was the only month in the year when all her garden owners were uniformly troublesome—wanting, to a woman, horticultural wonders done by June.

She looked round to remind herself of who had done the church flowers this week. Marjorie Marchmont, she decided without difficulty. She would have known even if she hadn't been keeping an eye on Marjorie's garden all the year round herself, fending off her vigorous forays into the flower border and making up for her equally taxing periods of total neglect, when something or someone diverted her attention from her plants.

No two people arranged flowers in the same way—Cynthia had a theory that flower arrangements were as individual as finger-prints—and the definiteness of Marjorie Marchmont shone through the firm reds and bright blues and the manner in which they were packed stiffly into the church vases.

The church door creaked and another mourner came in. Herbert Kelway, village grocer and unctuous with it. Half-currant Kelway was what he was called behind his back—his scales never went down too heavily on the customer's side—and he'd been known to chop a currant in two. He always came to his customers' funerals—and he liked to be known as a provision merchant rather than as a grocer. Cynthia Paterson, who didn't like him, didn't think he would be either for very many more years—he was losing trade steadily to the big self-service stores in Berebury and Calleford.

Peter Miller came in hard on the grocer's heels. He was a farmer and not losing out to anyone. On the contrary, thought Cynthia dryly. Peter Miller's land, Fallow Farm, marched alongside the Fent property and Fallow Farm had prospered mightily under his go-ahead new management. She wouldn't be at all surprised if Peter Miller were thinking of buying an acre or two of Strontfield Park if he got the chance. He'd be lucky, she thought. Nobody had had a chance to buy any Fent land for generations—and it wasn't likely that Peter Miller would be any luckier than anyone else.

The bell tolled again and at the same time old Nellie Roberts came in. No funeral in Constance Parva was complete without Nellie Roberts. Her place in the church was strategic and her office that of messenger—the Greeks, Cynthia was sure, would have had a word for it. From Nellie's pew both the lich-gate and the approaching *cor-*

tège were in full view. At the same time Nellie herself could be seen clearly by clergy and organist. Both were obedient to cues in the form of a nod of Nellie's time-battered straw hat.

At much the same time as Nellie Roberts took up her look-out station, so to speak, Cynthia saw Richard Renville and his wife, Ursula, enter. They joined Cynthia in her pew, Richard placing himself next to her, his wife on his other side.

"A bad business," he hissed in her ear.

She nodded, and whispered back, "Poor Helen . . ."

Richard Renville pulled down the corners of his mouth in a quick grimace. "And poor Bill . . ."

"And poor Bill," agreed Cynthia Paterson *sotto voce*.

Bill Fent of Strontfield Park who had gone to join his fathers.

Almost unconciously Cynthia Paterson tilted her head until she was looking at the Fent family tablets on the north wall. The thought, she decided defensively, wasn't as pagan as it first seemed. There on the church wall were memorials to his ancestors—there had been Fents at Strontfield Park long before anyone could remember—and now Bill's name would join those of his father and grandfather and all the other William Fents of Strontfield.

Her eye wandered over toward Bill's grandfather's name. He had died of pneumonia in the days when you did die of pneumonia. Cynthia could remember her own father praying in church that old William Fent would live through his pneumonia crisis—and he hadn't. Any more than Bill's father had lived to come back from Dunkirk in spite of all the prayers there were. Not, of course, that modern medicine—or peace—would have saved Bill Fent. He was dead before the ambulance got anywhere near him.

Everyone said so.

The other driver was still alive, though. The ambulance had rushed him hell-for-leather to Berebury Hospital. That

would be a simile left over from the horse, decided
Cynthia, her mind drifting away from the vision of Bill
Fent, dead, to that of a man lying unconscious in a hospi-
tal bed.

And like to die too, they said, though on what authority
she didn't know.

Her mind's eye could take in the intensive care unit at
the hospital because she had been there on its opening day.
She'd been invited because she'd been a collector for the
hospital in the old days when two pence a week and an annual fête seemed able to cover all the running costs—and
now she collected for the Friends of the Hospital for patients' comforts above and beyond the call of the Health
Service.

What had struck her then about the intensive care unit
had had nothing to do with the magnificent chromium and
electronic equipment of which they all seemed so inordi-
nately proud. It had been a matter of words. The words
hadn't even been on a door. Just on the plan, and in very
small print at that.

The non-recovery theatre.

She'd thought about those words since. There was one
thing to be said for gardening as an occupation: it left the
gardener with plenty of time for thought.

The non-recovery theatre was where they took the or-
gans for transplanting from the patients who hadn't got
better. It was medicine which was mealy-mouthed. Not the
Church. The Church didn't go in for euphemisms. On the
contrary. It rejoiced in plain words. There was nothing
equivocal about those in the Order of Service for the Burial
of the Dead in front of her now.

On the other hand, thought Cynthia fairly, it was medicine not the Church which went in for daring innovations
like transplants—it wasn't all that long ago that the Church
had stood in the way of medical progress. She—true gar-

dener that she was—was all in favour of transplant surgery. Lilac onto privet had been her own first success . . .

The church door creaked again.

It was all a bit like compost. Cynthia Paterson's train of thought was getting confused now but she knew what she meant. One of her own cardinal gardening principles was that anything that had lived once—be it paper, cotton, leather, wool—could live again as compost.

The creaking door had meant that someone else had entered the church. It was a woman and she found her way to a pew somewhere at the back of the church; but this time—for a wonder—Miss Cynthia Paterson, who knew everyone in the village, did not recognize who it was who had come in.

Detective Inspector C. D. Sloan recognized her.

Her name was Mrs. Mary Exley and Detective Inspector Sloan knew who she was because he had seen her before—the day before yesterday, to be exact. She had been at the inquest on William Fent and so had Detective Inspector Sloan. She had been sitting inconspicuously at the back, then, too. Part but not parcel of the proceedings, so to speak.

She was present at both the inquest and the funeral out of a strange courtesy. That was the only way of putting it. It was her husband, Tom Exley, who was lying at death's door in the intensive care unit at the Berebury District Hospital.

Inspector Sloan didn't need a second look at her to know that the poor woman could hardly have eaten or slept since last Saturday night when it all happened. He'd been in at too many deaths and bad accidents not to recognize the signs and symptoms—even if he hadn't already known that the inquest and funeral were the only two occasions that she'd left the bedside of the bandaged and betubed man—almost, so very nearly, a lay figure—that was her husband.

Detective Inspector C. D. Sloan (Christopher Dennis to his wife and parents, "Seedy" to his friends) was head of Berebury Division's tiny Criminal Investigation Department and in this capacity he didn't have to attend many funerals.

"You'd better go to this one, though, Sloan," his superior officer, Superintendent Leeyes, had advised. "You never know . . ."

"Yes, sir."

"Fire a shot across their bows and all that." Once upon a time, a long time ago, the superintendent had travelled briefly in a naval landing craft. From that day forward he had used the Navy's idiom as if he had been born to the sea.

"Yes, sir."

"And take Constable Crosby with you. He doesn't look like a policeman. Nobody would ever guess that he was"—Leeyes, normally dogmatic beyond the point of contradiction, looked up in need of reassurance—"would they?"

"No, sir." Sloan had been quite firm about that. "Never. He doesn't look in the least like a policeman."

The trouble, of course, with Detective Constable Crosby was that he was inclined not to behave like a policeman either, and this was a worry to his colleagues in the Force.

"The funeral might fill you in on the background a bit more, Sloan." The superintendent had rubbed his hands together like an undertaker. "Nothing like a funeral for finding out who's related to who."

"No, sir."

"A Will's better, of course. We haven't seen that, have we, Sloan?"

"Not yet, sir."

"Nothing on the books about him?"

"Just that he had a fire-arms certificate, sir. All in order. I checked. The local constable says he was a pillar of society down their way. Old Calleshire family, too . . ."

Superintendent Leeyes had snorted gently at that. "Doesn't mean a thing these days. When they're bad, Sloan, they're very bad indeed."

Gregor Mendel, the monk of Brünn, might have seen fit to agree with the superintendent. Sloan certainly didn't.

He shook his head. "No, sir. Our chap out in the village —P.c. Bargrave—was quite happy about him. He was on the Bench, too, you know . . ."

Leeyes's snort hadn't been quite so gentle that time. "All right, Sloan, all right, have it your own way. Either the deceased led a blameless life or death wiped the slate clean. Now, where does that get us?"

So far it had got Detective Inspector Sloan and Detective Constable Crosby precisely as far as the very back pew of St. Leonard's church, Constance Parva, just before noon on the morning of Friday, August 27th, for the funeral of one William Fent of Strontfield Park in the county of Calleshire.

The church door creaked again and again—and again. People were coming in more quickly now. Sloan caught a glimpse of the faintly familiar face of a local magistrate here and there, though he himself didn't ever have to appear before the particular Bench on which William Fent had sat—that was the Lampard one.

There were touches of decent black everywhere and a due solemnity about everyone's behaviour. All orders of society, noted Sloan, were represented—even, he thought ironically, the police.

Officially as far as the funeral was concerned they came in the person of Superintendent Bream of Calleford, who, if he recognized two plain-clothes members of the detective branch sitting at the back of the church, didn't reveal the fact by so much as the bat of an eyelid. Resplendent in the police equivalent of full canonicals—ceremonial uniform, gloves, cane and all—he too had come to pay a last tribute to one of Her Majesty's justices of the peace, dead upon the midnight the Saturday before.

Dr. Dabbe, consultant pathologist to the Berebury Group Hospital Management Committee, took a noticeably jaundiced view of road traffic accidents upon the midnight any night of the week but especially on Saturday nights.

"As bad as Tam O'Shanter's old grey mare, the lot of 'em after a drink or two," he had grumbled, mixing up his verse too. "Ready to see anything but the road. What happened this time?"

That had been—in the first instance, anyway—Inspector Harpe's province. He was in charge of Berebury Division's Traffic Department.

"Difficult to say exactly, Doctor," he said in his usual melancholy way. Inspector Harpe was known throughout the Force as Happy Harry on account of his never having been seen to smile. On his part he maintained that so far there had never been anything in Traffic Division at which to smile. "We reckon he took Tappet's Corner too wide."

The pathologist had nodded.

Inspector Harpe flipped over a report. "He hit another car coming the other way and ended up upside down in a ditch. The other chap's pretty bad but still alive."

"Was he alone?" The pathologist was used to multiple casualties nowadays. Motorways did that for you.

"What? Oh, yes. He was on his way back home to Constance Parva. They'd had some sort of dinner party at Strontfield Park and Fent had just taken one of the guests home to Cleete. A Professor Berry. An old boy. Retired. Terribly put out that it was because of him that Bill Fent was on the road at all at that time of night."

The consultant pathologist had nodded, scooped up the necessary papers, and gone over to the mortuary.

And he'd done a routine test for alcohol in the deceased's blood and found some but not a lot.

And done a routine post mortem to establish the exact cause of death and found poison as well.

TWO

"He won't actually call it poison, though," Police Superintendent Leeyes had informed Sloan when he had had Dr. Dabbe's report.

That had been on the Monday.

"Oh, no," he went on. "Poison's too strong a word for our precious pathologist so he doesn't use it."

"What," inquired Sloan cautiously, "does he say then?"

"A potentially injurious substance," trumpeted Leeyes scornfully. Never a man to mince words himself he could never understand anyone else doing it either.

"Ah."

"He says," continued Leeyes unappeased, "that during his examination he found evidence that the deceased had ingested . . . ingested . . . now there's another damn silly word . . ."

"Eaten or drunk," supplied Sloan, "and he doesn't know which."

Leeyes glared at him. "I know that." He straightened out the paper in front of him. "Now, where was I? . . . oh, yes . . . had ingested a compound which he believes may have had strong sedative qualities."

"Dope," said Sloan simply. He waved a hand expressively. "The stuff you give horses and neurotic women. When you're not giving them pep pills," he added.

"Either way," responded Leeyes tartly, "winner or loser, will do in a motor car."

"Yes, sir."

"Dr. Dabbe says," went on Leeyes, still consulting the

report, "that it may have been taken thera . . . thera . . . therapeutically . . ."

"As medicine."

"Or in excessive quantity."

"An overdose," translated Sloan, like all policemen and doctors more familiar with overdoses than he used to be.

"Or in a normal dose but with its effect potentiated—why the devil can't the man write decent English—by alcohol."

"Very likely." Sloan's experience was that alcohol potentiated everything—but especially motorists.

"But," Leeyes waved the report in front of him in Sloan's face, "driving under the influence isn't going to stick and it doesn't get us anywhere anyway because he wasn't."

"No, sir?"

"He says the blood level of alcohol as analysed by the gas chromatographic method is well below the legal limit. Nowhere near it, in fact. And that's without any playing about."

Sloan nodded. He understood that bit all right. No blowing into little bags, no little tubes turning colour, no engineered delays, no prevarication about taking blood—and, above all, no argument.

He coughed. "What about under the influence of drugs, sir?"

The superintendent slammed Dr. Dabbe's report down on the desk. "He won't say that for sure, either."

"Not until they've done a bit more analysing, I suppose . . ."

"Listen, Sloan. Quote: 'I cannot say with any degree of exactitude and without further examination' "—Leeyes savagely mimicked the precise language of the police pathologist—" 'the quantified effect of a substance alien to the body whose chemical and pharmacological properties have not yet been established.' "

"So that, sir . . ."

"Wait for it, Sloan. Wait for it." Leeyes might have been a sergeant on the parade ground. "That's not all. Listen to this bit . . ." He resumed his reading: "'. . . or the effect of a synergic or catalystic agent should either or both have been present in the body at or immediately previous to death.'"

There was a small silence.

"Either," said Sloan flatly, "he knows but he's not saying . . ."

"Or"—Leeyes glared across his desk at him—"he doesn't know and doesn't want to say so."

"There'll be things to analyse, won't there?"

"He's pickled some bits and pieces," agreed Leeyes graphically, "and put them in jars. It's all written down here. Stomach, liver, kidneys, and spleen. Anyway Constable King told us that much."

Police Constable King acted as coroner's officer and routinely represented the Division at post mortems ordered by the coroner.

"The coroner . . ." began Sloan.

"The inquest . . ." said Leeyes at the same instant.

The two policemen regarded each other for a long moment.

Then . . .

"I'll leave you to talk to the coroner," said Leeyes basely. "This half-baked stuff isn't evidence . . ."

Miss Cynthia Paterson could see at a glance how upset old Professor Berry was.

And no wonder.

He practically tottered into the church for the funeral, his gnarled veins standing out, knotted and blue, on his shaky old hands.

She felt very sorry for him. Not that any of all this could be said to be his fault. Bill Fent always took him home after a dinner party at Strontfield Park if no one else was going toward Cleete—just as he and Helen always asked her to come to dinner when the professor was invited.

He was a theologian and an old friend of her late father's rather than of hers, but she knew him well and in any case she'd long ago reached an age that was socially ageless. Just as, equally long ago, she'd reached a status that was socially neutral. She was just the old rector's daughter—everything and nothing, so to speak. She dined at the Park—to keep their numbers right—and took tea with the district nurse; she had the travelling county librarian to luncheon and gave the peripatetic teacher for the deaf a bed from time to time—and earned her living in almost everyone's garden.

The Washbys followed the professor in.

They, decided Cynthia Paterson, had probably brought him over from Cleete today. They had been going to take him home on Saturday night but at the last minute Dr. Paul Washby had had a call. He was the only doctor in the village—had been ever since he had succeeded old Dr. Whittaker—and Veronica was his new wife.

They—Paul and Veronica Washby—were much more of Bill and Helen Fent's age group than she and the professor. Veronica Washby was one of the prettiest girls Cynthia Paterson had seen in a long time. She was as pretty as . . . as a fritillary, decided Cynthia. The dinner party at Strontfield Park had been in her honour. Paul Washby's bride was being welcomed to the village and being introduced to Constance Parva.

Next but one to Cynthia in her pew, Mrs. Ursula Renville leaned forward to pick up a prayer book. Ursula Renville—middle-aged or not—was tall, graceful and indefinably elegant. Now she was more like a willow than a fritillary. No, willow was too substantial. Not willow. There was something else in the garden that Cynthia was reminded of . . . Ursula Renville was more like . . . like . . . she'd got it . . . like dierama pulcherrima. The wand-flower. Hanging mauve flower bells suspended from a slender arching stem. Not completely hardy, of course—but then that went for Ursula Renville too. And didn't like being moved when mature. You could say that, thought Cynthia silently, about pretty nearly every well-rooted inhabitant of Constance Parva.

The Washbys had settled themselves down in a pew beside Peter Miller, the farmer. You couldn't very well call it their usual place because they didn't come to church often enough for that. Oddly enough, Cynthia Paterson, true daughter of the rectory that she was, wasn't too sorry about this. Paul Washby, excellent general practitioner that she had every reason to suppose him to be, had more than a touch of Chaucer's Physician about him, and every gentle reader suspected *his* religious observance to have been mere form.

Cynthia Paterson knew her Chaucer better than most people. She'd read *The Canterbury Tales* aloud to her father time and again in his declining years when his eyes had begun to fail—and not in modern English either but sounding every syllable and last "e" in true medieval style.

The more she thought about it the more Paul Washby fitted Chaucer's bill of the man of medicine. Fonder of gold than he cared to let show, that good pilgrim had been ready enough to enter into a fairly unholy alliance with the Apothecary. And if the Plague had meant more work and therefore more money surely he hadn't minded about that dread disease as much as he should have done . . .

Caught up in a vision of a train of pilgrims in an earlier England her mind drifted away from the church again . . .

So did Sloan's.

His mind went back to when he'd seen the coroner for West Calleshire. It had been in the coroner's office in Berebury on Monday afternoon.

That worthy solicitor had been affable to a degree.

And he hadn't been born yesterday, either.

"I shall hold an inquest, Inspector, at eleven o'clock on Wednesday morning in the Guildhall," he pronounced as soon as he had heard Sloan out, "and the only evidence that I propose to take that day will be that of identification."

"Thank you, sir."

"Who'll do that, by the way? Not the widow, I hope . . ." He was a compassionate man.

"No, sir. Constable Bargrave has seen her, of course, but she wasn't keen. Still very shocked, he said. There's a cousin, I understand, though, who was staying there at the time. A Mr. Quentin Fent."

The coroner nodded and made a note. "And in the first instance, Inspector, I shall adjourn the inquest for one month."

"Thank you, sir. That would be a great help . . ."

"In the hope," continued the coroner blandly, "that the other injured party—I've got his name, haven't I? Ah, yes, Mr. Tom Exley—in the hope that Mr. Tom Exley will be recovered sufficiently by then to give evidence."

"Thank you, sir," said Sloan again, grinning to himself. There was no doubt that the coroner was as wily as they came—as befitted a man qualified in law who spent his days tangling with doctors.

"No point in rushing things, Inspector."

"None, sir."

"And we don't want any hares started, do we?" The coroner, mostly desk-bound, always thought of himself as a country solicitor.

"No, sir," agreed Sloan stolidly.

"On the other hand this does need looking into—just in case. We haven't got the full report yet, have we? Probably only his usual sleeping tablet stirred up a bit too much by a large nightcap." He grimaced feelingly. "The sort of one you'd need after a big dinner party."

"Could be," agreed Sloan. He and his wife, Margaret, did not entertain on such a scale. His own parents came to see that his wife was looking after him properly. His in-laws visited to check that his wife—their daughter—was being decently cherished. And that—so far—was all. Besides, semi-detached houses in suburban Berebury did not lend themselves to stylish dinner parties and Sloan's own nightcap was usually milky coffee. "We do know, sir, he wasn't expecting to have to go out again that night but Dr. Washby had a late call and at the last minute couldn't take another guest home. Fent took him instead."

"Quite so," said the coroner, making another note. "A month then, I think, would do very well all round. If there is anything more that I should know abut the post mortem, Dr. Dabbe and his analyst friends will have come up with it by then. And a month will do you?"

"I hope so, sir."

"After all, Inspector," he mused, "identification is really what inquests were all about. It was after the Norman Conquest they started having them."

"Really, sir?"

"You only had 'em at all to make sure that the dead man wasn't a Norman," said the coroner cheerfully. "If he was English it didn't matter."

"Fent was English all right, sir."

The coroner ignored this. "If he was a Norman, you see, the English had to pay a fine. Hence all the fuss about identification. You tried to prove your body wasn't Norman. Presentment of Englishry, it was called . . ."

Which was how it had come about that when the next batch of mourners entered the church the thoughts of Detective Inspector Sloan were rooted even further back in the past than those of Miss Cynthia Paterson.

Mr. and Mrs. Daniel Marchmont were among those who came in in that batch, and neither Sloan nor Cynthia Paterson, abstracted as they both were, overlooked the fact. Mrs. Marjorie Marchmont wasn't often overlooked. Her husband might have been. Easily. But not Mrs. Marjorie Marchmont. There was a natural ebullience about her, underlined by her large size, which even the circumstances of a funeral could not quell. And a child-like preoccupation with the present.

The first thing which she did, observed by both Sloan and Cynthia Paterson, was to consider the church flowers, and then to leave her pew to tweak a piece of wayward greenery back into place. Actually, Cynthia Paterson, no mean flower arranger herself, thought the arrangement much better as it was before but Marjorie Marchmont evidently felt it lent nothing to her decoration. She rammed the adjacent flowers even farther into the vase and then went back to her place.

What Sloan also noted was that—the family apart—all the guests at Saturday night's fatal dinner party were now assembled in the church. He ticked them off mentally: there should be eight. There was the professor—he'd seen him come in with the doctor and his wife, that was three; the Daniel Marchmonts, who'd just arrived—you couldn't miss her—must be fifteen stone if she was a pound—five; the Renvilles—now there was a good-looking woman—he didn't know what to make of them yet—seven; they were sitting next to the gardener woman—Miss Paterson—a proper village spinster if ever he saw one—that made eight.

They'd all assembled at Strontfield Park just before eight o'clock on Saturday evening. Bill Fent had died as near to midnight as didn't matter. Those were the only fixed points in time that Sloan had.

He'd done his level best to winkle a few more out of the pathologist. That had been on Tuesday. And it hadn't been easy.

"Sloan, I can't be expected to say for sure," Dr. Dabbe had said cagily, "when the deceased took whatever it was he did take until we know exactly what it was he took, can I?"

"No, Doctor." It was the only answer.

"All I've got to go on until I have the analyst's full report is that there was something there which perhaps shouldn't have been."

"No more than that, Doctor?"

"Not yet, Sloan. When we know exactly what it was he took . . ."

"Or had given," pointed out Sloan soberly.

"True. Your pigeon that one, of course," said the pathologist, who also fancied himself a countryman. "On my part . . ."

"Yes, Doctor?"

"I might go so far as to say that I think it was a narcotic that he'd taken; and that it was unlikely that he'd had it very early that evening or the effects would have been apparent before he set off to take the old boy home."

Sloan nodded.

"There's one more conclusion that we can draw while we're about it, Inspector . . ."

"Oh?"

"That if substance 'X' had emetic qualities . . ."

"Emetic?"

"Sick-making." Dr. Dabbe grinned. "If it did . . ."

"Then," concluded Sloan for him, "the deceased didn't take it until after dinner. I quite agree. We'd heard that he ate his dinner all right."

"Heard?" chortled Dabbe robustly. "I know for sure, Sloan. I had a look."

That slightly earthy aspect of the case was also troubling someone else.

By Sloan's side in the church Detective Constable Crosby stirred. Raw, brash, and the constant despair of the entire complement of the Berebury Police Station, the superintendent had been quite right about Crosby. No one would take him for a policeman. The constable's conception of "plain-clothes" was a piece of natty gent's suiting, and Sloan could only call his choice of a tie for a funeral conspicuously unsuccessful.

"Sir," he whispered now, "what will they do with the bits afterwards?"

"Bits?" inquired Sloan bleakly.

"His innards. The bits they put in jars. They aren't being buried today with the rest of him, are they?"

"I should hope not."

"Well, then . . ."

"If there's anything in them that oughtn't to be there then they'll be wanted as evidence and be preserved."

"For ever?"

Sloan sighed. "We could offer them to the Black Museum, I suppose . . ."

"And if not," persisted Crosby hoarsely, "will they have a special service for his liver and his lights or . . ."

Sloan never did hear Crosby's idea of a suitable alternative, and a sudden bob of activity on the part of Miss Nellie Roberts' straw hat saved him from having to take official notice of the question.

The organ music died precipitately away and—following Nellie's lead—the congregation got to its feet. Through the open door from the direction of the lich-gate could be heard the crunch of feet upon gravel and then, approaching the church porch, the firm voice of the present rector of St. Leonard's, Constance Parva, beginning the Order for the Burial of the Dead.

THREE

First on her feet was Miss Cynthia Paterson. She was
slightly ahead of Nellie Roberts' blue straw hat because
she'd been keeping her ear subconsciously attuned to
Gregory Fitch's minute bell. He'd stopped his tolling when
the *cortège* reached the church, his task done for the moment.

Just like the inscription on the bell said "Too the grave
do summons al" so Bill Fent had answered the summons
now.

Like Detective Inspector Sloan, she too noted that all
the guests who had been at the dinner party at Strontfield
Park were now in the church. From there onward her
thoughts were rather different.

Fellowship was the image which sprang to her mind.

Fellowship and Jollity to be precise.

Fellowship was a character in another piece of early liter-
ature to which her late father had been addicted in his
own old age—*The Summoning by Death of Everyman*.
More to the point than most sermons, but too strong for
modern congregations, as he'd often declared before going
down to the church to deliver a well-thought-out piece of
scholarship about the Hittites.

They'd all come to church today—the guests of Saturday
night. She wasn't surprised. She'd expected to see the Renvilles, the Marchmonts, the Washbys, and the professor
here. In the play Fellowship would only go so far with
Everyman when poor Everyman had to report to Death.
They—the guests—were Saturday night's Fellowship and

Jollity at Friday's funeral, who would also come thus far
and no further.

And now she came to think of it, Fellowship had been
the first of his companions on the way to desert Everyman.
Even Knowledge had stayed by his side a little longer.
Then Knowledge too had left him . . .

She heard the approaching funeral party reach the
church porch.

Kindred, Discretion, Beauty, Strength, and Five Wits
had all stayed with the allegorical Everyman for a while
and then gone, leaving him with only Good Deeds to sup-
port him in his rendering to Death.

Kindred, she thought confusedly, were still with Bill
Fent—would stay with him just a short while longer. They
would be behind the coffin. That would make Saturday
night's party complete.

Twelve. Fellowship, Kindred, and Everyman . . .

She turned her gaze toward the door and marked off Bill
Fent's kindred as they entered the church.

Helen Fent, Bill's widow, a dark-haired, intense woman,
pale but outwardly composed.

Or doped for the morning. You never knew these days,
though Cynthia herself never touched anything stronger
than aspirin . . .

Helen was being supported by Bill's cousin Quentin
Fent.

Then came Annabel Pollock, another cousin, looking
quite distraught and leaning heavily on the arm of an elderly man. An uncle on the mother's side, Cynthia Paterson
thought.

After them came the usual miscellaneous assortment of
distant relatives dredged up by a family funeral and made
prominent by occasion. They, decided Cynthia from her
vast human experience, would have come to Constance
Parva for the funeral and would go away again after the
reading of the Will . . .

The prospect of Bill Fent's Will being read that day had troubled Detective Inspector Sloan.

"I don't see why it should," Superintendent Leeyes had said testily.

"If someone did set out to kill him," protested Sloan, "they might benefit from his death before we could stop them."

"Come, come, Sloan, be reasonable," said Leeyes. "Even if we handed over the entire case to Detective Constable Crosby . . . which Heaven forbid," he added hurriedly, rolling his eyes upward in supplication, "I daresay even he would solve it before any lawyer we've ever known wound up Fent's estate—or anyone else's, come to that."

"Perhaps, sir, but . . ."

"Besides, we want to know what's in it, too, don't we? There may be big mortgages, attachments, and so forth on the property. To say nothing," added Leeyes, warming to his theme, "of sundry by-blows and what have you."

"Dead and never called him father?" suggested Sloan ironically.

"People say what they mean in Wills," said the superintendent. "About the only time they do, too."

"Even so . . ."

"Discreet inquiries, that's what we're supposed to be making, Sloan, in case either everything's above-board after all or we frighten off suspects. We're not supposed to be shouting the odds from the roof tops."

"No, sir."

"And if we stop them reading the Will there'll be hell to pay from Fent's solicitors for a start—invoking the law left, right, and centre, I expect."

"Yes, sir." In his more thoughtful moments Detective Inspector Sloan, policeman, liked to think of himself as an upholder of the law but this didn't seem to be the moment to say so.

"There's another thing, Sloan . . ."

"Sir?"

"If the press get hold of this too soon . . ."

Sloan nodded. He didn't need to say anything. If there was one subject in the whole wide world at which he was completely at one with Superintendent Leeyes it was the press.

". . . then," continued his superior officer, "the whole case would be blown wide open."

"If there is a case," Sloan reminded him.

"If there is a case. And if there isn't, Sloan, then where do we stand?"

"In trouble," agreed Sloan mordantly. "Up to our necks."

The superintendent poked a finger at the report on his desk. "He did die from a ruptured aorta . . . there's no doubt about that. That's the devil of it."

"The noxious substance was there," said Sloan. "At least, that's what Dr. Dabbe said." He paused. "I think."

Leeyes snorted. "A fat lot of help we're going to get from our friendly neighbourhood pathologist. I've had another go at him, by the way . . ."

"Oh?"

"You're not going to believe this, Sloan."

"No, sir?"

"Apparently," said Leeyes savagely, "poison is like beauty . . ."

Sloan waited.

"It's in the eye of the beholder," growled Leeyes.

"Never."

"That's what he said. How the poison acts is nothing to do with the law. Nor the result of the poisoning. It's all in the mind of the person who administers it."

"So even if whatever was there hadn't harmed him, if whoever gave it to him meant it to, then there's a case?"

"That's it."

Sloan considered this in silence for a moment.

The superintendent indicated the telephone on his desk. "I tried to ring him again a few minutes ago but he's not at the hospital. Gone out to look for a hair to split, I expect."

But Sloan was still thinking about Bill Fent. "Let's get this quite straight, sir. He died from injuries received in a road traffic accident . . ."

"Agreed."

"What we are checking on is whether someone tried to kill him first."

"Got it in one, Sloan."

"Which makes it attempted murder."

"Agreed," said the superintendent. "Or murder full stop."

"How come?"

"If he had the accident because of the poison."

"The lawyers are going to like this one, sir, aren't they?"

"Never mind about the lawyers," grumbled Leeyes. "They can look after themselves if anyone can. What about us?"

"I couldn't agree more," said Sloan fervently. "Give me a straightforward manual strangulation any day of the week. At least you do know where you are then . . ."

Sloan's discreet inquiries had already included a chat with Professor Berry, which told him nothing that he didn't know already, and a visit to Dr. Paul Washby's home and surgery.

"He still lives over the shop, sir," Crosby had observed as their car slipped into the village. "Real country stuff."

"Good." Sloan eyed the pleasant Georgian house in the middle of Constance Parva High Street with approval. "All the more likely to catch him at home."

"Mrs. Washby?" began Constable Crosby to the attractive young woman who opened the door. "We're . . ."

"I'm the receptionist," said the girl rather shortly. "Would you wait in here, please . . ."

When she had gone Sloan looked at the ceiling and remarked to no one in particular, "When I started in the Force they warned me never to shake hands with the butler."

The good-looking young woman reappeared. "Doctor is just finishing his afternoon surgery. He'll see you now. This way, please . . ."

"Just a quick word, Dr. Washby, if we may," began Sloan easily. The receptionist, he noted, took her time about leaving the room. "I've already seen Professor Berry because our Traffic Division have asked us to check up on one or two small matters arising out of Saturday's fatal accident."

"Quite so." Dr. Washby jerked his head vigorously. Country doctor he might be but there was nothing conspicuously rural about him. His suit was London-tailored and his manner far from bucolic.

"If," said Sloan, "the deceased was in good health and so on."

"As far as I know he was," Washby said. He pulled a desk diary toward him. "Will I be wanted at the inquest?"

"Not at this stage, Doctor, I don't think. You were his usual medical adviser, though?"

"Oh, yes." The doctor ran a hand through his hair. "Since I've been here, that is. And Dr. Whittaker—that was my predecessor—before me."

"Eyesight?"

"I don't think I'd ever examined it." Washby frowned. "But he never complained of anything being wrong—and he was a darn good shot."

"What about sudden dizzy turns—that sort of thing?"

The doctor shrugged his shoulders. "There again, not to my knowledge. Something like that might account for the accident though. Of course, you can get a dizzy spell from a simple digestive upset. You don't need to have anything really wrong." He pulled his lips down in a long grimace.

"God, Inspector, how I wish I'd taken old Berry home myself on Saturday night and then all this might not have happened."

"On the other hand," pointed out Sloan, "it still might."

"What? How?" Washby gave another quick frown. "I always take Tappet's Corner at snail's-pace myself. I've attended too many accidents there already. Rotten bit of road. Something should be done about it."

"I was thinking of the other driver," said Sloan.

"I was forgetting about him," admitted Paul Washby immediately. "Yes. He might well have hit me for six too. Us, actually. I had my wife with me. Could have been all his fault, when you come to think about it. Probably was. Fent was a good driver."

"Blame," remarked Sloan sententiously, "is always a difficult thing . . ."

"Especially when one driver is dead . . ."

"Especially when there's no junction involved," said Sloan sedately. It was surprising how much of Inspector Harpe's troubles rubbed off on the rest of the Force.

Washby nodded. "Quite so. And knowing won't bring Fent back again anyway."

"No." Sloan paused. "We did wonder, Doctor, if he had any special worries—something that might have impaired his concentration. We find as a rule that a lot of the drivers who have traffic accidents have something on their minds." This was Happy Harry's road credo again.

The general practitioner pursed his lips. "I shouldn't have thought he had. Not that I knew about anyway, There was the development, of course, but . . ."

"What development?"

"It hasn't happened yet. But it will, I expect. We had main drainage put in the village last year in spite of Miss Paterson and all the other old stagers who thought it was a pity. As soon as that happened the property companies started sniffing around." He gave a quick grin. "Sewer rats Cynthia Paterson and her cronies called them."

"And?"

"And they wanted to buy some of Bill Fent's land. It's about the only ground round here the planning people would give permission for because of its position near the centre of the village. Within the village envelope somebody told me—whatever that may mean." Washby grimaced. "Bill Fent couldn't sell because of an entail or something on the property and the property wallahs wouldn't lease—not enough money in that, I suppose, these days. They're not silly."

"I don't quite see what . . ."

"I know Bill was scratching around to see if he couldn't raise enough capital to develop it himself because he told me. I think he was a bit worried about that. After all he was saddled with that damn great Park to keep up and precious little to do it on."

"Did you give him anything for his worries?"

"I don't remember that I did." The doctor cocked his eyebrow inquiringly at Sloan. "I could check though . . ."

"If you would . . ."

Washby flipped a switch and leaned forward to speak into some sort of communications box. "Jean, bring me Mr. Fent's record, will you, please? Here we are. No. No, there's nothing down here, Inspector. I didn't prescribe anything for worry for him."

"What about for his wife?"

Washby hesitated. "I couldn't say, Inspector. Mrs. Fent is not a patient of mine. I believe she sees a woman doctor in Berebury but you would have to ask her that."

Sloan nodded comfortably. "That'll be our Dr. Harriet Baird, I expect. A lot of the ladies go to her."

Cynthia Paterson, lady gardener, turned her attention back to the principal mourners—those who would remain when the more distant connections had gone home.

Helen Fent, widow, Annabel Pollock, cousin, and Quen-

tin Fent, cousin. With Bill Fent, deceased, that had made
twelve on Saturday night.

There had nearly been one more. Cynthia Paterson had
been distinctly punctual that evening—in fact she had been
the first of the dinner guests to arrive.

"I know I'm too soon," she apologized to Bill Fent when
he answered the door. "That's the trouble with a bicycle."

"Beats the internal combustion engine any day," Bill
Fent had agreed solemnly. "Come in. We've got another
visitor. Peter Miller. I was just chatting to him about our
mutual boundary."

"Evening, Miss Paterson," said the farmer.

"There now," she said in confusion, "I'm interrupting
you both."

"I was just going," Peter Miller assured her, downing the
last of his drink. "Truly." He turned to Bill Fent. "Wasn't
I?"

"Well," Bill Fent had said gravely, "we'd settled that I'd
pick up some spiles from Greg Fitch first thing on Monday
morning and get something done about that fence."

"Good. Your shrubs aren't going to like my Jersey cows
any more than my Jersey cows are going to like your
shrubs."

"True," said Bill.

"Good fences make good neighbours," Peter Miller had
added sententiously.

"As long as you don't want the bounds beating again,"
said Cynthia Paterson brightly, her quick ear detecting un-
dercurrents. The two men facing each other looked
curiously alike in their controlled crossness. A bit like bantam cocks already squared up but trying not to fight.
"Young Tommy Pennyfeather hasn't got over his bruises
yet, I hear."

Both men had laughed and the moment passed.

"Quite sure you won't stay for dinner, Miller?" Bill Fent
asked as the doorbell rang again.

"Quite sure, thank you." Miller put his empty glass down, the ice still unmelted. "I must be off. Didn't mean to bother you on a Saturday evening anyway . . ." he added gruffly.

"I don't suppose," said Bill Fent more easily, "that even a prize herd of Jerseys as good as yours know the days of the week."

Miller grinned. "Not yet. Though they're real lovelies . . ."

"Just as well he didn't stay," said Bill when the young farmer had gone. "We'd have been thirteen at table. Helen wouldn't have liked that."

"No."

"Unlucky."

"Because of Judas," said Cynthia Paterson.

"Not that I'm superstitious myself."

"Of course not," said Cynthia Paterson. "It's just that you wouldn't actually want to be thirteen at table."

"Now you're pulling my leg." He paused on his way to the door. "I say—don't forget to tell Annabel you like her flower arrangements, will you? She thinks a lot of your opinion . . . and she's been at 'em all day while Helen saw to the food. Milly Pennyfeather's going to wash up for us."

But Cynthia Paterson hadn't liked Annabel Pollock's flower arrangements one little bit. And her dislike hadn't been anything to do with the way in which the flowers had been arranged. Annabel Pollock was an artistic creature, with a good eye for colour and design, and her floral arrangements were always a pleasure to look at.

It was their colours she didn't like. Red and white. No hospital sister would ever have them alone together in a patient's vase on her ward if she could help it. Mixed with other colours, yes. Just the two, no. Red for blood and white for death.

Unlucky. Annabel was a nurse and she should have known that.

Bill Fent's coffin had reached the chancel steps now.

"We brought nothing into this world," intoned the rector of Constance Parva in a Church of England quaver, "and it is certain that we can carry nothing out . . ."

Peter Miller might just as well have stayed at Strontfield Park on Saturday night, thought Cynthia Paterson, thirteen or not. Bill Fent couldn't very well have been unluckier than he had been.

FOUR

Sloan knew why it was that Crosby still had the deceased's anatomy on his mind at the funeral. It dated from their visit to the pathologist on his home ground. That had been on the Wednesday afternoon.

"Come in, Sloan, come in," Dr. Dabbe had called out cheerfully as the two policemen had knocked on the hospital laboratory door. "Welcome to our place of employment. It's Constable Crosby you've got with you, isn't it? Thought I knew the face. Come along in, boy. You'll find all this very interesting and it's all good experience." He waved a hand. "Now, this gentleman here is Dr. Writtle from the Home Office. He's an analyst."

The fourth man in the laboratory nodded formally to the policemen.

"I suppose I should remember to call you a chemical analyst, eh, Writtle?" said Dr. Dabbe.

"I'm certainly not a stock market one."

The pathologist grinned slyly. "Nor yet a psycho-analyst."

"God forbid," said Writtle fervently. "I like to know what I'm doing."

"And so say all of us," chorused Dabbe. "Well, what we're doing this afternoon is very interesting—come, come, why such a long face, Sloan?"

"I don't like interesting cases, Doctor," said Sloan stolidly. "Make a lot of work do cases that you people call interesting."

"Do you hear that, Writtle?" cried the pathologist. "Good job I'm not sensitive."

"You should try the Civil Service, Dabbe," said the analyst genially. "No use being sensitive there. We get blamed for everything. And the Home Office always cops what can't be pinned onto anybody else."

"All the same, Sloan," said Dabbe more seriously, "we do have a pretty little problem here. Haven't we, Writtle?"

"Very nice," agreed Writtle judiciously. "Mind you, Inspector, we shouldn't have had a problem at all if Dabbe here hadn't been wideawake. I can tell you that not every county pathologist would have spotted what he did at a routine traffic accident post mortem."

"Come, come, Writtle," protested Dabbe with due modesty, "anyone would have noticed those petechical haemorrhages on the pericardial surfaces."

"What about the loss of aeration in the lungs, then?" countered Writtle. "Very like the findings in ventricular fibrillation."

"True."

"I should say nine chaps out of ten would have put that down to primary myocardial ischaemia."

"Surely not."

"Especially if there was any narrowing of the coronary arteries."

Sloan coughed. "Gentlemen . . ."

"And that," added Writtle handsomely, "was before you got anywhere near the stomach."

"You must agree," pointed out the pathologist, "that he was a bit too young for too much ticker trouble."

"Exactly," exclaimed Writtle. "That's just what I mean. Not everyone would have remembered that the aorta can be hypoplastic with minimal atheroma in younger subjects."

Sloan smoothed out the pages of his notebook.

"Gentlemen," he said again, more loudly this time, "if we might begin at the beginning, please . . ."

Both men turned toward him.

"The stomach," said the pathologist promptly.

"The seat of all the humours," chipped in Dr. Writtle.

"Behold the stomach"—Dr. Dabbe produced a large sealed glass jar and slid it along the laboratory bench toward Sloan and Crosby—"otherwise known as Exhibit A."

Sloan took one quick look at the glass jar and then averted his eyes.

Crosby opened his eyes wide and vowed never to eat tripe again. Ever.

"I thought there was a distinct loss of tone in the stomach," said Dr. Dabbe. "What did you think, Writtle?"

"Definitely." The analyst pointed a bony finger at the contents of the jar. "No irritation of the duodenal mucosa, though. All of which does tend toward . . ."

"Quite," said the pathologist.

"The stomach . . ." said Sloan, beginning to write.

"Ah, Sloan, it was the liver that was really interesting," said Dabbe.

By what was apparently some sort of legerdemain another jar appeared as if from nowhere and came sliding down the bench. This one was labelled "B" and it came to rest in front of Detective Constable Crosby. Crosby swallowed audibly and began to babble about vegetarianism.

"All right. The liver, then," sighed Sloan, writing that down instead.

"The interesting thing about the liver," began Dr. Dabbe in a hortatory tone, "is that— I say, Inspector, your constable's gone a very funny colour all of a sudden. Are you feeling all right, boy? Hey, Writtle, catch him before he falls. Here, put him on this chair. Had we better put his head between his knees, do you think?" he asked anxiously. "I haven't had a live patient in thirty years, you know . . . never did like 'em when they could answer back. Wonder what could have upset him . . ." The pathologist peered round the hospital laboratory, which was lined from

floor to ceiling with gruesome specimens, saw nothing untoward, and took another look at Crosby. "Feeling better
now? Good. Now, Sloan, where was I?"

"We'd got as far as the liver being interesting," Sloan
answered him evenly. He tried not to look at Crosby. Sitting uneasily on a chair, his head sunk between his knees
and his face the colour of old putty, was no place for anyone detailed to assist him on an investigation of anything
stronger than a missing bicycle pump. The essential policeman in Sloan turned away from the unedifying sight.

"Oh, the liver was interesting, all right," said Dabbe.
"Very."

"In what way, Doctor?"

"The liver had more of the—er—alien substance in it
than the peripheral blood did," said the pathologist, "at
the same time, mark you, Sloan, as there was still some of
the same substance—whatever it was—in the stomach."

"I see, Doctor," said Sloan, "and that means . . . ?"

It was the Home Office analyst who fielded his question
this time. "When you have that situation, Inspector, it in-
dicates that death occurred before peak absorption and not
all that long after the substance had been taken."

"Ah," said Sloan, "and if death hadn't—er—occurred
when it did when might it have been expected to—er—have
occurred—if it was going to occur at all, that is?"

"We thought you'd want to know the time," said the
two scientists in unison.

"We've done some work on it," added Dabbe.

"But not all of it," said Writtle.

"Enough to be able to say . . ." began Dabbe.

"Only approximately, mind you," put in Writtle cautiously.

"Yes?" murmured Sloan gently. He did his best to sound
encouraging. At this rate they would be in the laboratory
all night and he didn't like it any more than Crosby did really.

The pathologist twiddled a pencil between his fingers.

"Assuming that no medical aid was summoned or happened to be to hand . . ."

Sloan said, "I think we can assume that, Doctor."

"And that no remedial measures were taken . . ."

"Yes?"

"Then I think our subject would have died . . ."

Sloan looked up. He'd forgotten that doctors who were forensic pathologists didn't have patients any more. Only subjects.

". . . some time during Saturday night," continued Dr. Dabbe. "What do you think, Writtle?"

Writtle stroked his chin. "I'm only an analyst, of course, but say between three and five o'clock in the morning . . ."

"There you are, Sloan," said Dabbe generously. "The dead of night. What more do you want?"

The rector, a weather eye on the chief mourners, had now got down to a brief eulogy of the late Bill Fent, tailored to the occasion. Miss Cynthia Paterson didn't listen too closely to the clergyman's valedictory tributes. She'd heard them all before. Besides, she was thinking about something else. She wasn't so absorbed, though, as not to be aware that Ursula Renville had been crying for some minutes or that little Veronica Washby, Paul's new bride, was very near to tears. Oddly enough Cynthia Paterson was glad about this—a tough doctor's wife was no help to any village.

Predictably Marjorie Marchmont remained dry-eyed. Cynthia knew that there wouldn't be so much as a sniff from Marjorie for all that she'd probably known Bill Fent better than any of them. And there never would be. She wasn't a person who could project her emotions beyond herself. Cynthia herself wasn't tearful either. Spinsters don't cry. She'd found that out long ago. When she'd discovered that there was no one to comfort a spinster's tears . . . Besides, being the rector's daughter had toughened her to death—or perhaps it was the gardener in her that made her so aware that everything which lived and grew and flowered had a mortal end.

The rector had reached the last Collect now and the undertaker's men moved forward . . . that was another change with the times, thought Cynthia. Time was when a coffin would be borne by men from round the deceased—work-mates, employees, friends, and relatives—a last tribute. That custom had died out too, along with bell-ringing. The men who came forward now were strangers to her and, she was sure, to the Fent family too. The men put their shoulders to the oak coffin, turned unsteadily, and began their journey back down the chancel.

The family followed.

Even as she averted her eyes from the sad little procession Cynthia wondered why she did so. What primitive feeling made one hesitate to look upon grief and fear when joy and anger were no trouble to watch? Her mind dawdled on the thought while she focused her eyes on the pulpit—on the reredos—on the Lady Chapel—anywhere where she could not possibly catch Helen Fent's eye. Opposites, she thought, firmly, were always intriguing. Her father had once preached on Giotto's opposites in the chapel at Padua.

She recounted them to herself as first the coffin and then the mourners passed by the end of her pew: Justice and Injustice; Fortitude and Despair; Temperance and Wrath; Prudence and Envy (a neat pair, those); Faith and Inconstancy; and Charity and Folly. A fine sermon those last two had made. That the medieval opposite of Charity should be Folly had intrigued the Reverend Wilfred Paterson no end . . .

The last of the family mourners passed out of sight and the atmosphere in the church relaxed.

Veronica Washby looked as if she might be able to get by now without actually crying. Ursula Renville gave a final convulsive sob and Marjorie Marchmont changed her mind about the flowers again. She stepped out of her pew and gave them another strenuous prod.

Of the men, Professor Berry looked old and sad, and Paul Washby slightly impatient. That came, she decided charitably, of his being a doctor. Daniel Marchmont—one always had to look twice to see where the self-effacing Daniel Marchmont had got to—was waiting for his wife to finish lashing the flowers into shape. Richard Renville, a considerate man if ever there was one, turned to Cynthia and chatted with her in an undertone, thereby giving his wife a little more time in which to collect herself.

"Tappet's Corner of all places," he said. "Bill knew it as well as anyone else round here. Better, probably."

"It's a bad bit of road, even on a bicycle," said Cynthia. "I sometimes get off there and walk myself."

"It always has been a bad bit of road," mused Renville. "My grandfather turned his trap over there once, though I must say he was on his way home from market at the time."

"Bill wasn't on his way home from market," remarked Cynthia.

"I know," said Renville, taking her meaning straightaway. "And he wasn't in a hurry, either. Now if it had been one of the Pennyfeather boys in a souped-up old banger I could have understood it. But not Bill. One of the best drivers this side of Calleford."

"And one of the best cars," added Cynthia temperately.

"What . . . oh, yes, of course. Nothing wrong with that, I'm sure."

"Then perhaps the other driver . . ." she suggested.

Renville shook his head. "Doesn't sound like it to me. Fellow in his middle thirties. Married with two kids. Steady sort of chap from all that I hear." Richard Renville himself was the sort of chap who always managed to pick up what information there was going. Some people were like that.

"It was a family car." Cynthia herself had heard that. "Not a sports model or anything like that."

Renville came near to a chuckle. "The car oft proclaims the man, you mean?"

"Doesn't it?"

"Perhaps it does," he conceded in a decorous whisper. "Time we changed ours and neither of us wants to. A pair of stick-in-the-muds, the Renvilles of Constance Parva." He slipped his hand under his wife's arm as she made a movement toward the aisle. "Aren't we, dear?"

Ursula Renville nodded mutely.

Cynthia Paterson waited a moment and then stepped out of the pew herself. She found she was standing between the young farmer Peter Miller and Herbert Kelway.

"This is a sad day for Constance Parva," said the grocer. "They don't come like our Mr. Fent very often."

"I certainly couldn't have had a better neighbour," added Peter Miller with an emphasis Cynthia thought was intended for her.

She found a phrase in reply which had stood her in good stead after many a funeral. It fitted into those awkward moments when it didn't seem permissible to speak except of the deceased, but when everything else about them had already been said.

"His sun went down while it was yet day," she murmured.

All of the congregation were standing now, and Detective Constable Crosby was using his position at the very back of the church and his height—well above minimal police regulation—to survey the rest of the mourners. He studied the backs of their heads one by one so hard that, irritated, Sloan whispered to him.

"Is your middle name Lombroso, then, Crosby?"

"No, sir," he whispered back. "Edward." There was a pause. "Who's Lombroso?"

"An Italian chap who thought you could tell a bad 'un from the set of his ears."

"Oh." There was another pause. Then, "And can you?"

"Not that I know of," sighed Sloan. "It's not as easy as that."

He wished that he had Sergeant Gelven with him today instead of Constable Crosby. Gelven was a policeman to his finger-tips—to his finger-prints, you might say—and sturdy, reliable, and resourceful into the bargain. And, of course, it showed.

"First time I've looked for villains at a funeral, sir," Crosby resumed his chatty whispering.

"They may not be here," said Sloan, though he didn't believe that himself. Everyone who had had anything to do with the Fents' fatal dinner party was at the funeral—right down to the village grocer who supplied Strontfield Park and the neighbouring farmer who had called in at the house before the party.

"Sure to be, sir," Crosby hissed back confidently. "It's always family or friends who do you in . . ."

Sloan grunted. Ninety per cent of the time it was, too.

". . . and they'd be here anyway," continued Crosby. "Up front."

"All right, all right," he said. "I promise we'll start with the kith and kin as usual." Sloan allowed his gaze to travel to the pews nearest the coffin, his thoughts not so far removed from those of Miss Cynthia Paterson after all.

"Nearest and dearest, that's who it'll be, sir, I bet," pronounced Crosby with all the airy assurance of the young.

"I'll make a note," said Sloan solemnly. "A hundred to one?"

"Unless it was a pure accident," qualified the constable quickly.

"There's no such thing as a pure accident, Crosby," responded Sloan in a firm undertone, "and the sooner you get that idea into your head the better."

It had been Inspector Harpe of Traffic Division who had
taught Sloan that. There were only two sorts of accidents,
the melancholy Harpe insisted after half a lifetime's study
of every untoward incident and accident in the county of
Calleshire. There were, Happy Harry always said, ignorance accidents and going-somewhere-to-happen accidents,
but never, never simon-pure accidents.

"Besides, Crosby," Sloan added for good measure,
"whatever it was the deceased swallowed in the way of an
injurious substance didn't affect anyone else, did it?"

"No, sir. Not that we know about." It had been Crosby's
job since Monday to cultivate Milly Pennyfeather who had
been in the kitchen at Strontfield Park on Saturday, and to
begin quietly to check the other guests and the family for
disquieting symptoms.

They hadn't had any.

Sloan too had done a good deal of unobtrusive asking
around since the pathologist's report had come in. Nothing
he had established so far had been the slightest help . . .

There had not even been anything useful to be gleaned
from the rector's funeral oration. Like Cynthia Paterson
he'd been around too long to be influenced by them anyway. Unlike Cynthia Paterson he always remembered that
bit about a man not being on oath when he rendered them.
And clergymen were only men. That was something else
you found out after a year or so in the wide world too.

Sloan didn't know what effect the rector's well-chosen
words had had nearer the front. They had certainly made
at least one back-bencher restive: the one standing next to
him. It was just as well that the two policemen were right
at the back of the church because Constable Crosby's
hoarse whisper wasn't anything like quiet enough.

"We're like a couple of mosquitoes in a nudist colony,
aren't we, sir?" he hissed cheerfully. "Our trouble is that
we don't know where to begin."

FIVE

"That's where you're wrong, my lad," said Sloan, but he did not say it aloud.

As far as Sloan was concerned the case had already begun. It had started for him in Dr. Dabbe's Pathology Laboratory on Wednesday afternoon, the day that Dr. Writtle had been there and Crosby had turned queer. No wonder that the constable chose to forget it.

"The dead of night," the pathologist had said. "What more did you want, Sloan?"

In the event Detective Inspector Sloan had wanted more —much more—from Fair Science than just the postulated time of William Fent's death without the intervention of the motor car.

"I need to know exactly what Fent took for a start," he had replied, "and in what form." By then he was glad to see that Crosby was beginning to sit up and take notice again.

"Here we are, Inspector." Writtle, the Home Office analyst, tapped two smaller bottles and sent them scurrying down the laboratory bench to join the stomach and the liver which had so upset Constable Crosby. "These should tell us what could have done the damage."

Both bottles were of dark-coloured glass. Sloan was relieved to see that they appeared to contain only some sort of powder. Even Crosby should be able to regard them with equanimity.

Dr. Dabbe grinned. "Whatever you like. Gog and Magog?" he suggested. "Or William-and-Mary—no, not

William-and-Mary"—he peered round the shelves of specimens—"I've got a hermaphrodite worm here some-where called that."

"Mutt and Jeff," croaked Crosby.

"He's feeling better," said the pathologist kindly. "What about Tweedledum and Tweedledee?"

"Antimony and Cleopatra?" contributed Dr. Writtle with a sly smile.

"It wasn't, was it?" said Sloan. "Not antimony, I mean?"

"'Fraid not, Inspector," said the analyst regretfully. "Nice pun if it had been, though. No, what we found was a barbiturate of a sort . . ."

"Ferdinand and Isabella," interrupted Dabbe irrepressi-bly. "I'm sure they looked alike, too."

"Tom and Jerry," offered Crosby. He was back to his normal colour again now.

"One of the free barbiturates," said Writtle. "That is to say, not a sodium derivative."

Sloan waited for enlightenment.

The analyst pointed to the two bottles. "Those crystals have been extracted by ether and chloroform. If we make an aqueous solution of the residue of one of them . . ."

"Gog," said Dr. Dabbe.

"And," went on Writtle, "then add one drop of Millon's reagent we get a white gelatinous precipitate which is proof of the presence of a barbiturate."

"Proof positive?" inquired Sloan. There was no word more loosely used than "proof" . . .

"It'll stand up in court," said Writtle, "if that's what you mean. Especially with the other one."

"Magog," said Dr. Dabbe helpfully.

"When a trace of that one is dissolved in chloroform," said the analyst, "and a one per cent solution of cobalt ace-tate added, you get a strong violet colour."

"'The dew that on the violet lies,'" murmured Dr. Dabbe poetically, "'mocks the dark lustre of thine eyes.' Sir Walter Scott. A neglected poet."

Crosby perked up upon the instant. "'Roses are red, violets are blue, sugar is sweet and. . . .'"

Then he caught Sloan's eye and his voice died away.

"How," inquired Sloan gamely of Dr. Writtle, "was the barbiturate administered?"

Crosby he could and would deal with later but there was absolutely nothing a mere detective inspector could do about a forensic pathologist with a bizarre sense of humour.

"In what chemical form, do you mean, Inspector? Probably in solution." The Home Office analyst, at least, Sloan was glad to see, was still on the job. "It might just have been in a highly soluble uncoated tablet but we doubt it. The main thing is that it wasn't in a capsule."

"We looked for one," said Dr. Dabbe.

"There was no sign of there having been a capsule," said Dr. Writtle. "There was no gelatine present anywhere in the alimentary canal."

"And it couldn't have gone far anyway," added Dabbe cheerfully. "Not in the time."

"Ah, yes, gentlemen," said Sloan. "The time. When . . ."

Writtle riffled through some papers. "It's not all that easy to say, Inspector, especially if the substance was administered in solution . . ."

"And perhaps in something he only sipped slowly," interjected Dr. Dabbe, "from time to time—say a liqueur—over half an hour or more."

"But we should be prepared to go so far as to say, Inspector," said Dr. Writtle, "that it wasn't—er—taken much before eight o'clock or much later than eleven."

Sloan wrote that down and noted the laboratory numbers from the bottles, and then turned over another page in his notebook. "The barbiturate—how much was there of it?"

"Good question," said Dr. Dabbe.

"Enough," replied Writtle, "to make sure that he didn't see morning. I'll let you have the full quantitative analysis on paper."

"Thank you, Doctor." Sloan looked from one to the other. "I think you've told me everything I need to know to begin with except one thing . . ."

"What's that?"

"Whether he took it himself or had it given to him."

"Another good question," observed Dabbe.

Writtle stroked his chin. "That's more difficult to say, Inspector."

"Your department, anyway, Sloan," said Dabbe mischievously. "Not ours. We're only the humble legmen, aren't we, Writtle? Hewers of detective wood and drawers of forensic water."

"And," went on Sloan crisply, refusing to be drawn, "whether, if he did take it himself, it was on purpose or by mistake."

"Ah," said Writtle thoughtfully.

"Or, come to that, gentlemen, if someone else gave it to him by mistake."

"We don't know that either, Dabbe, do we?" said Writtle.

The pathologist turned a look of bland innocence in Sloan's direction. "We know hardly anything about anything."

"I have heard," said Sloan firmly, "of cases where a person having taken a sleeping tablet is a bit confused by its effect. Then he can't remember if he's had his tablet or not and so he takes another."

"Automatism," said Writtle. "That's the name for that."

"And then he takes another tablet after that one," agreed Dabbe, "to be quite sure he's had his dose. It happens."

"Not as a rule until the patient is either in or near to going to bed," pointed out Writtle. "And not before setting out on a drive."

"He didn't know he was going to have to go out in the car," Sloan informed him absently. "Do I take these bottles away with me now, Doctor?"

"These? Oh, no, Inspector. These are only half our workings. We're keeping the other half with these meantime."

"For the Defence," added Writtle.

Dr. Dabbe waved a hand at the collection of specimen jars on the laboratory bench. He was quite serious now. "But that barbiturate, Sloan . . ."

"Yes?"

"I should say that it could constitute 'a destructive thing' within the meaning of the Act." The doctor looked at him. "What you need now for a watertight case is the 'malice aforethought' bit."

It was half an hour after they left the church before the chief mourners got back to Strontfield Park. Half an hour in which the coffin had been lowered into the grave, the rector had spoken the words of the Committal, and the funeral cars had driven back through the village. As they passed, Herbert Kelway lifted the blinds of his shop-window and then got back to work.

Back at the house duty called, too.

If Mrs. Helen Fent wanted nothing more than to shut herself away in her room she did not say so. Instead she moved slowly around among those present, politely responding to well-meant condolences. Always pale-faced, she was now almost without colour at all. She had chosen to wear a loose-fitting linen dress in a shade of charcoal

grey which went well with her raven hair but which also
served to heighten her pallor. She wasn't tall but even so
she stood out in the present company because people fell
back a little as she moved. In deference to grief, no one's
back was turned to her.

Like stage royalty, thought Annabel Pollock involun-
tarily, making her own escape to the dining-room. Cold
luncheon had been set out there by Milly Pennyfeather for
those who wanted it. Annabel busied herself twitching
table napkins into shape, adjusting a fork here and there,
and feverishly counting plates, even though there was really
nothing more to be done.

After a while, though, duty called her, too, back to the
drawing-room. There were relatives to be attended to, and
Nanny Vickers to be comforted. Nanny Vickers did not
like to see any of her charges—grown men or not—slipping
through her fingers.

"Thought I'd lost him once with the croup," she sniffed,
"but I pulled him through. Then there was mumps and
whooping cough. You were always a sickly one, too, Miss
Annabel. Came of being born and brought up in India, I
suppose."

"I know." Annabel was apologetic. "All those years in
the heat."

"He was a fine boy by the time I left." In Nanny
Vickers' view life's hazards were mostly over by the age of
twelve. "I never thought to see him go like this."

"No," Annabel Pollock agreed. "We none of us did."

"Cars!" snorted Nanny Vickers. "I wish they'd never
been invented."

"Amen to that," said Annabel, passing on to speak to
Great-Uncle George, a sprightly octogenarian, who'd left
the sheltered comfort of the private hotel where he lived to
come to Constance Parva for the funeral. Both Annabel's
and Bill's mothers had been his nieces.

"Annabel, my dear, why did it have to be Bill of all people? A mere boy with everything ahead of him."

Annabel Pollock nodded miserably.

"And here's me," went on Great-Uncle George, "eating m'head off and no mortal use to man nor beast at eighty-five—I don't look it, do I?—and as fit as a flea. M'doctor says," he added with every evidence of satisfaction, "that they'll have to shoot me in the end."

Annabel smiled wanly, and patted his arm. She'd noticed before now that the very old took death better than you might think—better than the young, anyway. Other people's deaths, of course, not the prospect of their own.

She passed politely on to Cousin Hettie, a more distant connection still, who had travelled to the funeral by bus and taxi from some ridiculously remote corner of the county—Almstone or somewhere like that—and who would presently have to be got back there. She'd been jilted, Annabel knew, long before Bill or she had been born and she'd promptly retreated to the backwoods and devoted herself to animals. They never rejected a human hand—particularly if it was the one which fed them.

She was regrettably inclined to sentiment.

"Such a nice boy," she lamented. "I thought he and Helen would have so many happy years together, didn't you?"

Annabel assented bleakly.

"I remember their wedding so well. They seemed the perfect couple—and now this. And no children either. Such a pity."

"Yes," said Annabel stoically. Perhaps if she listened to Cousin Hettie poor Helen would be spared the ordeal.

"You were a bridesmaid, dear, weren't you? So pretty in blue, you were. I've never forgotten. I see Helen's only in grey today. I know I'm old-fashioned but I do like to see the widow at least in black. Things aren't what they used to be, you know, dear. In my young day a widow was expected to . . ."

Annabel steered the conversation firmly toward Cousin Hettie's animal kingdom. Out of the corner of her eye she could see Helen talking to Mr. Puckle, the solicitor, and Quentin having his share of Great-Uncle George.

"Holiday," Quentin was saying firmly to Great-Uncle George, and he could be heard clearly across the room. Fit as a flea Great-Uncle George might be, but only if fleas were more than a little deaf.

"What's that?"

"I came down for a holiday," repeated Quentin, adding in an undertone, "and found myself 'super visum corporis.'"

Annabel Pollock heard him, even if Great-Uncle George didn't: Quentin Fent being clever at everybody else's expense as usual.

"What's that, my boy?" asked the octogenarian again.

"I always come down in August, Uncle. Nobody buys pictures in August." Quentin Fent worked for a West End firm of art dealers. He was some years younger than his cousin Bill, and rather precious.

"Should have thought you'd prefer the continent at your age," said Great-Uncle George.

"Can't afford it." Quentin gave the sort of winning smile that had sold many a picture to a hesitant client. It cut no ice at all with Great-Uncle George.

"Not married yet, are you?" commented the octogenarian with all the candour of the old.

"Not yet. The lady's father—er—won't have me."

"I didn't think anyone asked him any more," grunted the old man.

"He's Battersby's Bearings," murmured Quentin as if this explained everything. "Jacqueline's his only daughter."

Great-Uncle George heard that. "Ah, he thinks Botticelli's a cheese and that you don't know 'A' from a bull's foot."

"Er—exactly," agreed Quentin ruefully. "There's another thing too. He started out without two pennies to rub together. Now he thinks anyone who needs more than two pennies to get started is a bit of a failure."

The old man grunted unsympathetically. "In my young day you'd have . . ."

"I might have stood more of a chance," went on Quentin, "if I hadn't tried to change a wheel when Jacqueline and I had a puncture last month . . ."

"Made a mess of it, did you?" he remarked, unsurprised.

"The jack slipped." The corners of Quentin's mouth curved downward dolefully. "Had to call out the heavy recovery people. That set me back a bit, too. The worst of it was that we'd borrowed the old man's car without asking."

Great-Uncle George snorted. "So it was Strontfield Park for you, was it? Instead of Florence . . ."

"I like to keep in touch with the family," said Quentin a trifle defensively, "and believe you me, I'd rather do it in the summer." He looked round the large cool drawing-room. "You can keep your Christmas in the country. You'd never believe how cold this room can get in the winter."

"Oh, yes, I can," snapped the old man crisply. "I knew this room a long time before you did, don't forget. Came here first when my niece Mary married Bill's father. Before the war. Only coal fires in those days, too."

Quentin ducked. "Sorry. Of course you did. Must have been worse then." He steered the conversation hastily in another direction. "Rotten thing to happen on holiday— Bill being killed, I mean. Hell of a nice fellow."

"Steady as a rock," said Great-Uncle George, a quavering note creeping into his old voice.

"Straight as a die," supplemented Quentin, adding *sotto voce*, "and he died." He moved away from the old man to-

ward Helen Fent. "Hey, Helen, just a minute! There's
something I wanted to ask you. Something important."

"What is it?" Helen had completed her progress round
the drawing-room. She was standing now in front of the
Quare clock that had been her husband's pride and joy,
still talking to Mr. Puckle, the family solicitor. In spite of
the heat of the day she looked cold and remote. She passed
her tongue over dry lips and spoke without interest as
though to a child. "Did you want something, Quentin?"

"Yes. I want to know why there were policemen at the
funeral."

"Policemen at the funeral?" echoed Helen, sitting down
rather suddenly on the sofa. "Were there?"

Everyone in the drawing-room at Strontfield Park
stopped talking.

"Two," said Quentin.

"Bill was on the Bench, remember," said Annabel
Pollock quickly. "They must have known him quite well."

Helen's face cleared. "Oh, that would be Superintendent
Bream from Calleford."

"Not him." Quentin shook his head. "I meant
policemen in plain clothes from Berebury. Sitting at the
back of the church."

The silence in the room became more noticeable now.

"How do you know?" asked Helen between dry lips.

"They were at the inquest. The same two. They sat at
the back there, too. I asked Mr. Puckle who they were
then."

"And who were they?" asked Annabel Pollock breath-
lessly into the silence.

Mr. Puckle cleared his throat. "Detective Inspector
Sloan and a young detective constable, Miss Pollock. I
don't know his name. I—ahem—leave most of the Court
work to my junior partners these days. I'm a little out of
touch with the—er—Force in consequence."

"Not from Calleford at all then?"

"Oh, no," said the solicitor. "Inspector Sloan is head of Berebury's Criminal Investigation Department. Granted, it's not a big one. Anything of—er—great criminal moment is referred to the County Constabulary Headquarters at Calleford." He turned as a small sound came from Helen Fent's direction. "But I don't think that . . ."

She didn't hear him.

She had fainted.

SIX

Cynthia Paterson had been persuaded to go back to luncheon with the Renvilles after the funeral.

"It's very light." Ursula Renville sketched a gesture in the air with her long delicate fingers. "Just some soup and cold meat—I left it all ready before I came out. I didn't think we'd be hungry after all this . . ."

"Well . . ."

"There's plenty, though, Cynthia. Do come." She shivered slightly in spite of the heat. "Richard's got to go back to his office afterwards. Come back and stay with me for a while."

"What about Professor Berry? Hadn't I better see if . . ."

"The Washbys are looking after him." Ursula Renville peered round vaguely. "Veronica told me. And taking him back to Cleete afterwards."

"Good," said Cynthia, making up her mind. "Then I'd be delighted. I'll just let the dog out for a run and then I'll be round. By the way, Ursula, was that call of Paul Washby's on Saturday night anything important? I haven't heard of anyone being really ill."

Ursula Renville gave her friend an indulgent smile. "Cynthia Paterson, when will you stop being the rector's daughter? Whatever it was that was wrong there's no need for you to rush round with calves' foot jelly any more."

"I just thought you might know," said Cynthia mildly. "That's all."

"As a matter of fact, I do." Ursula Renville could no

more resist the challenge of implied ignorance than the next woman. "Veronica Washby mentioned it because it was all so odd. I wonder," added Ursula inconsequentially, "why calves' foot jelly was supposed to be so good for you."

"What was odd about the call?"

"The whole thing." Ursula was unenlightening. "Perhaps they're full of vitamins."

"What are?"

"Calves' feet."

Cynthia demanded detail about Paul Washby's call.

"Well, in the first place it wasn't a proper message, you know."

Cynthia said she didn't know.

"Not a person-to-person message and not a written message," elaborated Ursula. Theories of communication by other media—non-verbal or otherwise—had not yet reached Constance Parva. This was not to say that news did not travel throughout the village with the speed of light.

"What then?" asked Cynthia patiently.

"Just something on that funny answering machine the Washbys have got now. You know, it's never been the same since Marjorie left." Before the advent of Daniel Marchmont four years ago Marjorie had been secretary and dispenser to old Dr. Whittaker.

"Ah." Cynthia Paterson had not herself tried conclusions with the surgery answering machine, but she'd heard of plenty of people who had. "You won't catch that girl they've got there now—Jean Whatsername—sitting in by the telephone on a Saturday evening."

"No. Well," said Ursula, "before he left Strontfield Veronica rang back to ask the machine if there were any messages . . ."

"And the machine said yes," Cynthia finished the sentence for her. "I was there too, my dear."

"So you were," said Ursula with unimpaired serenity. "I was forgetting. Where was I?"

"Telling me about the message for Paul."

"Oh, yes. The machine said something about someone being taken queer over at Copway Street in Cullingoak—only it was a bit indistinct—and would the doctor go when he got back."

"It can't have been very urgent then."

"Oh, no. Paul leaves the number where he is on the machine for the patient to ring direct if it's urgent. I know that because Veronica doesn't like it. It means that anyone in the village can ring up and find out where they are for the evening."

"Poor girl," said Miss Paterson dryly. "Does she still imagine that they wouldn't know otherwise?"

"She's from London. I don't think she knows much about the country yet. It was a whirlwind courtship, remember. Anyway, when the Washbys got over to Cullingoak—which as it happens couldn't be farther from Cleete . . ."

"The exact opposite direction actually."

"Veronica said Paul couldn't find the place. He knocked up Mrs. MacArthur at the Post Office and she didn't know of anyone being ill."

"She usually knows," agreed Cynthia with the respect due to a usually reliable source of information.

"Not this time. Paul hunted about a bit but all seemed quiet. No houses with too many lights on or anything like that. It's not really part of his practice area, though he's got a couple of patients in Copway Street. They were both all right so he and Veronica came home."

"Didn't Paul run his machine through again when he got back?" inquired Cynthia intelligently. "I'm not sure how they work but . . ."

"He tried to," said Ursula, "but apparently poor Veronica hadn't left the switches set properly."

"She *has* got a lot to learn," drawled Cynthia ironically, "hasn't she?"

"When he tried to listen again the message had gone. She must have rubbed it out when she heard it the first time at Strontfield. Apparently you can . . ."

"It all sounds most unreliable," said Cynthia firmly. "When I want a doctor I want to be able to tell him so."

Ursula Renville regarded her lean stringy friend with something akin to affection. "When you want the doctor, my dear, we'll all get ready for another funeral. You're one of the tough ones."

"No," Cynthia corrected her. "Just old-fashioned. But I promise you I shan't put any messages on any machine."

"They're always finding odd things on it," said Ursula elliptically. "Very odd, some of them."

"I'll bet they are."

"They reckon it's boys playing about."

"I daresay it is," said Cynthia realistically. "There's very little for them to do in the village in the evenings."

"Boys and Mad Matthew. I'm told he finds it a great comfort. He thinks the doctor's listening to him all the time. In fact, what with the boys playing about and the machine being so sympathetic to poor Matthew . . . Oh, that's one of the things you shouldn't do, isn't it?"

"What is?"

"Endow an inanimate object with human characteristics."

"I must say Paul's answering machine doesn't sound exactly inanimate to me."

"No, but . . ."

Cynthia smiled. "You're right. Strictly speaking you shouldn't."

"I remember that from school. Funny what you remember and what you forget. You don't seem to have forgotten anything, Cynthia."

"Nonsense, Ursula."

"The Greeks had a word for it, didn't they?" persisted Ursula.

"Anthropomorphic," supplied Cynthia knowledgeably, "but I shouldn't let it worry you."

It was later at Strontfield Park. Dr. Harriet Baird had been summoned hastily from Berebury to deal with Helen Fent's fainting attack. Annabel Pollock, nurse, and Cousin Hettie, animal-lover, had tended her until the lady doctor had arrived and persuaded her, willy-nilly, to bed.

"The Will," murmured a wan, protesting Helen. "Mr. Puckle was just going to read it."

"Men!" declared Dr. Baird roundly. "Just like them to want the Will read at a funeral. Barbaric custom, if you ask me. Should be stopped. Well, they'll just have to get on with it on their own, m'dear. You're staying in bed . . ."

In the drawing-room Mr. Puckle smoothed out the thick legal paper in front of him, not sorry that the widow was not present.

"The provisions of the Will are quite simple, ladies and gentlemen," he began. "It was drawn up by me on Mr. Fent's instructions on the occasion of his marriage . . . that would be . . . let me see now . . ."

"Eight years ago," said Annabel Pollock. "They had been married eight years. I was still at school."

"Er . . . precisely." Mr. Puckle's attention went back to the Will. "Eight years. Acting upon my advice at the time" —he paused fractionally and regarded the assembled company over the top of his glasses: there was obviously a special limbo reserved in a lawless hell for those who did not take Mr. Puckle's advice—"Mr. Fent agreed to the insertion of the usual commorientes clause."

"Come again?" interjected Quentin.

"Commorientes," replied Mr. Puckle repressively. "Quite a customary measure in these days of high estate duty. It is a provision that before they can inherit the legatees shall survive the testator for thirty days."

"The family that travels together, dies together," murmured Quentin flippantly.

Rigid disapproval of this remark emanating from every muscle in his body, the elderly solicitor crackled the Will between his fingers and began reading. "'This is the last Will and Testament of me, William Anstruther Fent, of Strontfield Park, Constance Parva, in the County of Calleshire, Justice of the Peace . . .'"

Someone in the drawing-room let out a long breath. It did seem as if the solicitor was getting near the point now.

"As I said before," went on Mr. Puckle, "the provisions of the Will are quite simple. A certain proportion of the unsettled estate is to be set aside in trust to provide a life income for the—er—widow."

"Poor Helen," sniffed Cousin Hettie.

Mr. Puckle, liking neither flippancy nor sentiment, cleared his throat purposefully and continued. "Miss Annabel Pollock is to receive the deceased's moiety from his late mother's estate."

"My niece Mary," said Great-Uncle George gruffly. "A lovely girl."

Annabel lowered her head. "That was very nice of him."

"The entailed property," went on Mr. Puckle with some formality, "that is to say the estate held in desmesne, the messuage known as Strontfield Park and all other hereditaments in the schedule referred to in the Will of the late Captain Fent, who was entitled to the property in his own lifetime . . ."

"What's that?" Great-Uncle George cupped a hand to his ear. He only heard words that he understood. "What's that? Speak up, man."

"The settled estate," said the solicitor a trifle louder. "It passes under the original Deed of Settlement on the property to William Fent's eldest surviving son . . ."

"But," blurted out Annabel, "they didn't have any children."

"Failing live male issue," said Mr. Puckle austerely, "it devolves on the testator's nearest male heir at law of the whole blood."

Great-Uncle George pointed a bony finger. "That'll be young Quentin here, I suppose."

"So I suppose too," said the lawyer dryly, "but it will have to be established in the proper manner before the estate passes to him."

"My father," said Quentin to no one in particular, "was Bill's father's younger brother."

"Quite so," said Mr. Puckle, going back to the Will. "I should, of course, make it quite clear that the property passes under the terms of the original settlement—that is to say it cannot be sold or otherwise disposed of without the mutual consent of the owner and his heir-at-law who must be of legal age except"—it seemed that qualifications came automatically to the legal mind—"insofar as the provisions of the 1921 Trusts Act apply"—he took a breath and qualified this still further—"or, shall we say, could be construed as applying."

"And what happens," Quentin wanted to know, "if I should . . . well, you know . . . kick the bucket and all that within thirty days?"

"Ah"—the lawyer coughed—"should you be established as heir and then be so—er—unfortunate as to die within thirty days of last Saturday you would be—er"—Mr. Puckle searched for the *mot juste* and apparently found it—"er—deemed not to have inherited."

"Then what would happen?" asked Quentin curiously. "Not that I'm not feeling perfectly fit at the moment and all that."

"The entailed estate would then pass directly to the next male heir at law whoever he might be."

"Hector Fent," said Annabel Pollock promptly. "Bill's father's youngest brother."

"If he's still alive," said Quentin.

"Why shouldn't he be?" the solicitor inquired. "If he was the youngest of the three brothers of that generation he would not be a great age even now."

"Because," cackled Great-Uncle George, "he went to the bad years ago. Not on our side of the family," he added with a certain amount of relish.

"I've never seen him," said Quentin. "He went out to Australia after the war. Sheep farm or something, my father used to say. Queensland, I think. Back of beyond, anyway."

"Nevertheless," said the solicitor, "if he were still alive he would inherit if—er—anything happened to the present legatee."

"And if he isn't?" asked Quentin tightly.

"His sons if he had any." Mr. Puckle cleared his throat. "It . . . ahem . . . wouldn't be the first time a young man on an Australian sheep farm found himself the owner of an English estate."

"What if Hector died without sons, then?" persisted Quentin. "He wasn't married when he left England. Not that the family knew about anyway."

"Then," said Mr. Puckle in no whit put out, "we should have to search for the sons and grandsons of Mr. Fent's grandfather's brothers." He regarded Quentin over the top of his glasses. "You are aware, Mr. Fent, that we may have to institute a search for them anyway."

"Oh?" Quentin frowned. "Why?"

"As I explained earlier the consent of the next heir is required before you could realize any of the settled assets."

"Good Lord!" Quentin's face fell quite comically. "I hadn't thought of that."

At Berebury Police Station, Detective Inspector Sloan reported on the funeral to Superintendent Leeyes.

"Seemed a perfectly ordinary affair to me, sir. All the dinner party people were there and most of the village too, at a guess. All present and correct, in fact, you might say, sir."

"There's nothing correct about it," snapped an exasperated Leeyes. "Just stop and think what would have happened if the deceased hadn't had that car smash or Dr. Dabbe hadn't spotted the dope."

"He would have died hereafter," murmured Sloan under his breath.

"We might never have known about it, that's what would have happened," the Superintendent swept on unheeding. He had days when he seldom waited for an answer or heard one if it was given. "And then where would we have been? Tell me that, Sloan, tell me that . . ."

Sloan opened his mouth to speak.

"In the soup," said Leeyes for him.

"About the soup, sir . . ." Sloan seized the slender opening as quickly as he could.

"Soup?" echoed Leeyes testily. "Who said anything about the soup?"

"You did, sir."

"What? Oh, yes, so I did. Well, what about it?"

"We've found out something about the soup."

"Ah!"

"From our point of view, sir," said Sloan, permitting himself a rare moment of frivolity, "the soup of the evening was—er—beautiful."

"Are you having me on, Sloan?" Superintendent Leeyes looked up suspiciously. "What was beautiful about it?"

"Every single person at that dinner party at Strontfield Park on Saturday night—all twelve of them—drank it. There can't have been anything wrong with the soup."

SEVEN

"There was one thing about the soup which was rather odd, though, sir," continued Sloan.

"Well, get on with it, man! What?"

"It was cold."

Leeyes grimaced. "That happens in our canteen too, Sloan. Everyone has their off days."

"No, I didn't mean that, sir . . ."

"The guests stayed too long over their sherry, I expect," said Leeyes largely, "or had another glass and the hostess couldn't get 'em through into the dining-room in time."

"No, sir. The soup had never been hot."

"Never been hot? Why not?"

"It was meant to be cold soup," said Sloan.

"Funny idea, that, Sloan."

"Yes, sir. Can't say the thought appeals to me very much either."

Leeyes frowned ferociously. "What sort of soup?"

"Er—cucumber, sir," said Sloan, adding hastily, "after that they had roast crown of lamb and something called crémets."

"And what may that be when it's at home, Sloan? Fish, flesh, fowl, or good red herring?"

"Pudding, sir."

"Know anything about it?"

"No, sir, except that they had raspberries with it."

"Well," said Leeyes helpfully, "don't waste any time asking our canteen cook about it. If you can't boil it dry, she won't know. Soup, lamb, and crémets—that all?"

"There was cheese for those who wanted it."

"I should think they'd all want it after a meal like that," remarked Superintendent Leeyes, who took good care of his own inner man. "Drink?"

"Yes."

With exaggerated patience Leeyes said, "Not did they drink, Sloan, but what did they drink."

Sloan opened his notebook and read out carefully, "A wine called Dienheimer Falkenberg Spätlese 1964 Rhein-heissen, we think."

"How did you get that?"

"I didn't, sir." Sloan hesitated. "Constable Crosby did."

"Crosby? How come?"

"I understand," said Sloan sedulously, "that it was on Tuesday night."

"What's that got to do with . . ."

"Before the dustbins were emptied."

Leeyes let out a long groan. "He didn't take them? Not that . . ."

"Five green bottles," said Sloan. "All empty."

"Without a warrant?"

Sloan nodded.

"Theft during the hours of darkness," intoned Leeyes gloomily. "Does his mother know he's out?"

"He said he thought it might be helpful."

"A fine thing to happen," moaned the Superintendent. "A constable of mine coming up before the beak for theft during the hours of darkness."

"He wasn't seen." Sloan offered a crumb of comfort.

Leeyes went on keening. "It's enough to make my old station sergeant turn in his urn."

"He said he happened to be out late and thought he would see what he could see."

"You didn't give him permission, I hope."

"No, sir."

"That boy's still wet behind the ears."

Sloan looked up at the ceiling and observed thoughtfully, "It *is* easier than half the Force going through the Corporation tip on their hands and knees though."

Leeyes grunted.

"And not finding anything," added Sloan.

Leeyes paused and then he said, "Sloan, those five green bottles . . ."

"Sir?"

"Anything in 'em?"

"Just the dregs, sir."

"And nothing in the dregs that would help us?"

"No, sir."

"Anything on them?"

"Finger-prints, you mean, sir?"

"Yes."

"The deceased's and others not yet identified."

"You'll have to make Crosby your chain-of-evidence officer in the case, Sloan, then. You do realize that, don't you? He's the only one who can depose where those bottles came from. We might get by that way . . . otherwise they'll have to be lost. You understand that, Sloan, don't you?"

"Perfectly, sir."

"The rest of the meal," he growled, "how did you find out about that?"

"There was a young person employed that evening up at the Park to help with the washing up. Name of Millicent Pennyfeather. Crosby has been—er—chatting her up this week."

"At least," said Leeyes, "he hasn't done any breaking and entering to get at the larder. I suppose that's something."

"If," said Sloan, "he sees much more of her we'll have her mother after him wanting to know if his intentions are honourable."

"Coo-ee! Coo-ee! Ursula, where are you? It's me, Marjorie."

The Dalmation dog at Ursula Renville's feet stirred,

lifted its elegant head inquiringly, and then sank back into torpor.

"We're in the garden," responded Ursula. "This way." She and Cynthia Paterson were still drinking their coffee in the old loggia under the shade of the wistaria. "We're being ever so lazy sitting here. We haven't moved an inch since luncheon."

"I'm coming. Ah, there you are." Heavily overweight and very hot, Marjorie Marchmont stomped round the corner of the house. "I thought I might catch you out here in this heat."

"Come and sit down, Marjorie. Funerals do take it out of one, don't they?" said Ursula. "Coffee?"

"Thanks. Hullo, Cynthia. I didn't know you were here too." Marjorie flung herself down in one of the wickerwork garden chairs. Its semi-godetic construction took the strain better than many a drawing-room chair would have done. Even so, it winced visibly at the extra weight before it re-aligned itself—with creaks—to take the new stresses. "I must say, it's nice to sit down again. My poor knee's been sore all day."

"I'm not surprised. Look at what it has to carry about," said Cynthia with friendly candour.

"Daniel wouldn't like me thin," she said, bending forward to rub the offending member. "That's better. I think I'll have to have some more of that famous balm of yours, Cynthia."

"With pleasure." She grinned. "Though you were supposed to be the dispenser."

"Not any more. I've forgotten all I knew. Besides, I don't know what you put in it . . ."

"That's a trade secret."

"Well," admitted Marjorie a little grudgingly, "it certainly helped last time."

"You and your potions, Cynthia," chided Ursula Renville. "A couple of hundred years ago and you'd have been burned as a witch."

"A couple of hundred years ago," remarked Marjorie Marchmont pertinently, "if you were, someone might have wondered if you'd put your curse on the Fent family."

Cynthia looked up. "In what way?"

"Well," she said, "they've still got the same old trouble again up at the Park, haven't they? The trouble that they've always had."

"What's that?" Ursula asked her cautiously. Marjorie's thought-processes were deceptively simple, and needed taking one at a time.

"Getting rid of the entail. They're right back where they started, aren't they? Now that Bill's gone . . ."

"I suppose they are." Cynthia Paterson sipped her coffee thoughtfully. "They could always hunt out Hector Fent's sons if he had any . . ."

"He'll have had sons, all right," declared Marjorie robustly, "but whether he ever married their mothers is a different matter."

"He certainly had a twinkle in his eye," said Ursula unexpectedly. "I used to think he was the most handsome man I'd ever seen."

"He may still be alive," said Cynthia. "We don't know that he's dead. He wouldn't have been all that old, you know, even now. About our age, Ursula. Older than you, Marjorie."

"Ah," said Mrs. Renville, "but he will have lived."

"Ursula, really!" Cynthia regarded her friend in astonishment.

"Well, Constance Parva isn't really living, is it, Cynthia?" She set her coffee cup down on the rustic wooden table. "I don't mean that I'm not content or anything like that, and I'm very fond of Richard, but it's hardly life with a capital 'L', is it?"

Marjorie Marchmont hooted with laughter. "Ursula, you are a dark horse. Here you are, cherishing dreams of a tall dark handsome man in the Australian outback and all the while we thought wild horses wouldn't drag you away from the village and Richard."

"Still waters run deep," she said demurely. "More coffee, anyone?"

"Of course," said Cynthia Paterson, her mind still on the question of the Fent entail, "should Quentin and Hector or Hector's sons if he had any and has died himself since—should they get together the outcome might be just the same as when Bill and Quentin did their talking."

"And from all that I heard," said Marjorie expressively, "that was no go."

Detective Inspector Sloan—after talking to Mr. Puckle on the telephone—was trying to explain the same situation to Superintendent Leeyes. It took longer.

"What I want to know, Sloan," that worthy demanded, "is who gets the Strontfield Park outfit now? All that land must be worth a bit."

"Quentin Fent, cousin of the deceased."

"Then?"

"Quentin's sons, if he has any. After that, Hector Fent, uncle of the deceased. Last heard of in the backwoods of Queensland. Went out there after the war. The story is that he had an adventurous time until 1945 and then couldn't settle down afterwards. Bit of a black sheep, from the sound of things."

"Ha!" said Leeyes alertly. "A remittance man, I'll be bound."

"I couldn't say, sir, I'm sure. There is some doubt about whether or not he's still alive."

"He'll be alive, all right, Sloan. Only the good die young. And believe you me a remittance man lives longer than most people."

"Really, sir?"

"No worries," said Leeyes cynically.

"The Fents have had worries," said Sloan. "I've found out that much so far. According to the family solicitor there's an old-fashioned entail on the place. They've been trying to break it for years."

"They have, have they?" said Leeyes, sitting up and taking notice. "Go on."

"Apparently, sir," Sloan consulted his notebook, "it takes two to break an entail."

"Like it takes two to make a quarrel," said the superintendent irritably. "I know that. Get on with it."

"The deceased's grandfather died during the minority of his son—that would be Captain Fent's father—and Captain Fent himself was killed while his son—that's our William Fent—was still in short trousers."

"And the deceased—our William Fent—didn't have a son anyway, let alone one of twenty-one," finished Leeyes for him.

"Precisely, sir. This entail can only be broken with the consent of two adults."

"Don't talk to me about consenting adults, Sloan," snarled Leeyes. "It upsets me. You know that."

"No, sir. Sorry, sir." He took a deep breath and started again. "What the Fents have needed for a long time has been an heir who has been of age."

Leeyes pounced. "This cousin—Quentin Fent—he's the heir, isn't he?"

"Heir at law, I think." Sloan frowned. "He was heir presumptive all the while Bill Fent was childless. Or was it heir apparent? I'm not sure which."

"Presumptive or apparent," said Leeyes flatly, "isn't he of age?"

"Just."

"Well, then . . ."

"That's the interesting thing, sir. He—er—wouldn't consent to breaking the entail."

The superintendent glowered across the table. "Let's get

this quite straight, Sloan. Something kills off the grandfa-ther . . ."

"Pneumonia, sir."

"And the father."

"The Germans, sir."

"And our chap."

"The motor car, sir."

Leeyes let that pass. He said, "That happens soon after the heir presumptive or that other thing . . ."

"Apparent."

"Apparent—soon after he comes of age."

"Yes, sir."

"How soon?"

"A couple of months. Not of age, exactly, sir. The deed of entail specifies twenty-one years of age."

"Quite right, too." The superintendent didn't hold with the new coming of age of eighteen. "What was good enough for the Normans, Sloan, is good enough for me."

"The Normans, sir?" inquired Sloan politely.

"Didn't you know, Sloan? They put the age of majority up to twenty-one. From fifteen. Ten sixty-six and all that." The superintendent was given to attending evening classes and was the possessor of much sundry and totally unrelated information. "Norman armour and Norman horses were too big for Saxon lads of fifteen to handle so they put it up to twenty-one."

"Really, sir?" Sloan turned his attention back to his notebook. It was all very well for the superintendent and the coroner to be talking about the Norman Conquest but a lot had happened since then and he had work to do.

"So," continued Leeyes ruminatively, "young Quentin wouldn't renounce his rights."

"Asked for time to think about it, sir, according to Mr. Puckle."

"And," inquired the superintendent sarcastically, "had he done his thinking before this unfortunate accident?"

"I couldn't say, sir, I'm sure."

"Well, find out then, Sloan. Find out."

"Feeling a bit better now?" asked Annabel Pollock encouragingly. "I've brought you some fresh tea. I thought that would be better than coffee."

"Thank you." Now that Helen Fent was propped up on her pillows, her colour had begun to come back a little. "Wasn't that silly of me?"

"Of course not," responded Annabel warmly.

"I can't think what came over me."

"It might have happened to anyone. It's hot enough. Besides, you've had a terrible week."

Helen took a sip of tea. "I can't believe that it's only a week. Seems like a hundred years since last Saturday."

"Doesn't it?" Annabel's gaze fell upon the empty twin bed beside Helen's. She changed the subject. "I like your lady doctor, Helen. By the way, she says you're to stay here in bed until she comes again."

"But what about . . ."

"Doctor's orders," said Annabel Pollock. "Nurses can't go against them."

"Patients can," said Helen Fent briefly.

"Another cup?" asked the nurse, ignoring this. "And then I'll give you a hand into a nightie and you can get into bed properly."

"No." Helen pulled the eiderdown protectively up to her chin. "No, thank you, Annabel. I can manage perfectly well on my own, thank you. And I don't want to see anyone—do you understand?—anyone at all. Are they still here? The crowd downstairs . . ."

"Everyone's gone now except Quentin. Mr. Puckle wants to see him again on Monday in his office so he's going to ask you if he can stay on a bit instead of going back to town."

"Of course." A curious expression came over Helen's face. "We've got a lot to talk about—Quentin and I."

"I'll tell him."

"But," she added urgently, "I don't want to see anyone else—do you understand?" She grasped Annabel's arm. "Anyone at all—whoever they are. You're not to let anyone come upstairs to see me—whatever they say."

EIGHT

The tea which Detective Inspector Sloan and Detective
Constable Crosby drank midway through the afternoon
was only cousin many times removed to that served to Mrs.
Helen Fent at Strontfield Park. The dark strong Indian
brew of the Police Canteen bore little resemblance to the
faintly brown, tarry-flavoured Lapsang Souchong brought
to the bedroom by Annabel Pollock. And the buns which
came up with it for the policemen were notable for their
substance rather than their flavour.

Sloan was contemplating a report, chewing the while.

Crosby was finishing off a telephone call. "That was the
coffin shop, sir . . ."

"The what, Crosby?"

"Sorry, sir. The hospital. The Intensive Care Unit actually. I got the staff nurse this time. No change. Exley is still
deeply unconscious. His wife's back there again with him.
Her sister is looking after the kids." He took a bun,
regarded it critically and then bit into it. "I reckon," he
said after a mouthful, "that they get these buns second
hand from the railways."

The report on Sloan's desk was from Police Constable
Bargrave, who was stationed at Constance Magna but
whose wide country beat included the village of Constance
Parva. P.c. Bargrave had dutifully committed to paper all
that he knew of the twelve at the dinner table. It wasn't
encouraging reading for a detective.

"Do you realize, Crosby, that half of those people at

Strontfield Park on Saturday night could lay their hands on barbiturates if they had a mind to?"

"Dr. and Mrs. Washby, anyway," agreed Crosby, "for a start."

"And the girl Annabel Pollock, who is a nurse at St. Ninian's"—Sloan waved the report in his hand—"and Mrs. Marjorie Marchmont, who used to be a dispenser, and therefore presumably her husband, to say nothing of the gardener woman . . ."

"Miss Paterson? How come, sir?"

"You will be interested to know," said Sloan heavily, "that Miss Cynthia Paterson has a well-established local reputation in the village for being a dab hand at herbal remedies. Brews them herself, according to Bargrave."

Crosby started to count on his fingers. "That leaves the professor . . ."

"Who might very well have had sleeping tablets prescribed for him by his own doctor . . ."

"And the two Renvilles," enumerated Crosby, "then there's young Quentin Fent . . ."

"And the widow," Sloan reminded him. "Don't forget her."

"She hasn't anything to gain though, has she, sir? It sounds as if she even loses the house now."

"Beware of widows," said Sloan automatically. "Besides, according to your Milly Pennyfeather Mrs. Fent fainted when she heard that there were police at the funeral."

"The heat?" suggested Crosby, who had been told about the faint when he had nipped over to Constance Parva to ask Milly out that night.

"It's been hot all the week."

"The funeral?"

"The funeral was over."

"The Will?"

"The Will has been cut and dried for eight years. And the widow must have known all about the entail, seeing as how pretty nearly everyone else in Constance Parva seems to have known all about it too. Anyway, old Mr. Puckle reminded her of the provisions of the Deed of Settlement beforehand. He's just told us that. It turned out that she knew 'em already."

"I'd faint too, sir," said Crosby, "if I thought that long-haired art dealer chap with the fancy tie thing . . ."

"Cravat," said Sloan distastefully, "or jabot. I don't know which." Sloan himself only went out without a collar and tie on Sunday mornings when he went into the garden to tend his roses, and since his marriage he'd affected a decent sports shirt for gardening.

"If I thought he was the one who was going to have the jam off the bread and butter," said Crosby, "I shouldn't like it at all."

Sloan murmured thoughtfully, "He must be pretty glad all the same that he turned down the deceased's efforts at breaking the entail. Otherwise he might have lost out."

"As it is, sir," agreed Crosby, going on from there, "he's got all the dibs instead of only what the deceased would agree to."

"Except," Sloan reminded Crosby in much the same way as Mr. Puckle had reminded Quentin Fent, "he himself is now bound by exactly the same conditions as hog-tied William Fent in his day."

"I hadn't thought of that."

"Neither, I suspect," said Sloan dryly, "had our Quentin."

"What about this Australian uncle, sir . . ."

"You're going to find out all about him, Crosby," said Sloan briskly. "Send a request for information to the Police Commissioner, Queensland State Police. Somewhere down under may be the next male heir after Quentin Fent."

"Yes, sir."

"And find someone who can talk to me about this development that Fent couldn't afford. Someone sensible who knows what he's talking about."

"Yes, sir. Anything else, sir?"

"Plenty. See if you can get hold of that Home Office chap—Dr. Writtle—and find out if the barbiturate that Fent had could be a do-it-yourself job—you know, 'eye of newt, and toe of frog, wool of bat and tongue of dog.'"

"Sir?"

"Forget it. Just ask."

"Yes, sir."

"And Crosby . . ."

"Sir?"

"What else about this case bears looking into?"

Crosby screwed up his face in an agony of concentration.

"Come on! Something else you extracted from your friend Milly Pennyfeather. Don't you remember? Something about Saturday night."

The agonized look disappeared and was replaced by a triumphant one. "The telephone call!"

"Exactly. What we need to know is if that call was a put-up job—getting Fent out on the road at that time of night—or if it was a genuine call and Bill Fent was supposed to be overcome in the wee small hours at home in his own bed."

"Someone would have had to ring the doctor's number after the doctor had left his house for Strontfield Park," said Crosby.

"That wouldn't have been too difficult to arrange, surely."

"No, sir, it wouldn't but"—Crosby scratched his head—"it might not have been the only call for the doctor on the tape. Whoever rang would have to take a risk on there being other messages on it which would help us pinpoint the time."

"True. All the same you might ask Milly tonight if she saw any of the guests or family nip out to use the Strontfield Park telephone."

Crosby shook his head. "I did, sir. The only person she knew who left the others in the drawing-room apart from the Fents was Dr. Washby. He came out to the kitchen to give Milly her grandfather's tablets. For his heart."

"Before dinner or after?"

"Before. She was struggling to get that crown of lamb thing out onto a serving dish at the time. Had both her hands full. So the doctor just put them on the kitchen dresser and went back to the company."

"I see." Sloan wrote something in his notebook. "We're not getting very far, are we? We don't know if Bill Fent was the intended victim."

"No, sir. We don't."

"We don't know if the phone call for the doctor was a fake to get Fent out on the road."

"No, sir."

"We don't even know where the barbiturate came from."

"And," Crosby capped this recital of woe, "we don't know how whoever gave it to him actually got it into him."

Sloan abbreviated that for his notebook into the one word "opportunity."

"Or why, sir. We don't know that either . . ."

"He was on the Bench. We might just look back to see if anyone he'd sentenced had got it in for him."

"Yes, sir."

"And see if anyone of the party was in the habit of taking sleeping tablets." Sloan tried to make another note in his book but the ball-point pen wouldn't work. He threw it down on his desk. "I don't know about the buns but I think we must get our pens second hand from the Post Office."

The tea being served at King's Tree House, Constance Parva, by Mrs. Ursula Renville was China and better than that which came out of the Police Canteen urn. It was Earl Grey's.

"And very nice, too," said Marjorie Marchmont, who always appreciated food and drink in any shape or form.

"We should have gone ages ago," said Cynthia Paterson.

"No," said Ursula, "don't go yet. Do stay, both of you. Then it won't seem so long until Richard gets home."

"I must say, it's very comfortable out here in the shade." Marjorie leaned back in her chair and sipped the tea. "Daniel's gone off already. Back to work and then the Reunion."

"I wonder what will happen about the development now," said Ursula Renville. Actually there seemed no risk of either of her visitors leaving. Both of them were well and truly settled in the loggia. The Dalmation dog had gone to sleep.

Marjorie said, "It looks as if you might have won your fight to keep the village a village, after all, Cynthia."

Cynthia Paterson shook her head. "Lost it altogether now, I should say. Young Quentin doesn't look like a preservationist to me."

"Of course," said Ursula vaguely, "he may find Hector Fent and get him to duck out of the entail."

"That's right, I must say," snorted Marjorie Marchmont. "If he wouldn't do it himself for Bill why should he expect someone else to do it for him."

"Because," explained Cynthia reasonably, "Hector Fent —if he's alive—isn't really ever likely to inherit himself."

"And Quentin always stood a sporting chance, is that it?"

"In the natural course of events, yes." Cynthia had known Majorie too long to be put off by her manner. "He was younger than Bill by quite a bit, you know."

"Steady on," said Marjorie roundly. "Bill was my age exactly. We used to play together."

"I haven't forgotten." Cynthia smiled. "I remember you then quite well. Your hair was long then. You had pigtails nearly to your waist."

"It's longer now only it doesn't show," said Marjorie complacently. "I never have it cut. Just pinned up."

"I can see that it was worth Quentin's while to stick out against breaking the entail," said Ursula, her mind still on the Fents, "and not Hector's. But what if Hector has sons?"

"Ah," said Cynthia, "then that would be a different kettle of fish unless . . . until . . ."

"Until Quentin has a brace of sons in his quiver," Marjorie answered for her, giggling a little. "That's what you mean, Cynthia, isn't it?"

"It would alter the situation yet again," agreed Cynthia decorously.

"I learned that in Sunday School," said Marjorie unexpectedly. "About full quivers, I mean."

"There's nothing like the Bible for plain-speaking," responded Cynthia.

"I wonder what Helen will do now?" intervened Ursula. Cynthia and Marjorie—once started—were quite capable of arguing for hours.

"If she's got any sense," declared Marjorie, "she'll clear out. It won't be much fun for her watching Quentin lording it up at Strontfield."

"Pity there's no Dower House," remarked Ursula.

"There's always Keeper's Cottage," said Cynthia. "That's been empty since they took old Fitch away."

Marjorie sniffed. "It's not very big."

"It's big enough for one," said Cynthia. "One person doesn't need a lot of room."

"That's true," said Ursula. "It's the men who take up the space."

Marjorie roared with laughter. "Not in our house, it isn't."

"You'll really have to do something about your weight one of these days, Marjorie," said Cynthia eyeing her dispassionately. "Extremes in nature are always ill-favoured. You should know that."

"This development, then," Ursula intervened again, "what do you think will happen now? Richard'll be interested naturally."

"Nothing," said Marjorie promptly. "Quentin won't be able to sell and the property company won't lease. Stalemate."

"You've forgotten the third alternative," said Cynthia.

Marjorie looked up challengingly. "What's that?"

"For Quentin himself to develop as owner."

"What with?" asked Marjorie. "Peanuts?"

"That's the whole trouble actually, Cynthia," explained Ursula. "I thought you understood that. The Fents haven't a lot of money, you know. Never have had. Not that sort of money, anyway. Keeping a house like Strontfield going must have taken every penny Bill had."

"I know that," said Cynthia, undisturbed. "I wasn't thinking of Fent money."

"Not a mortgage," said Marjorie. "I know Bill tried that because he told me, but the mortgage people or whatever you call them . . ."

"I call them usurers," remarked Cynthia, "but then I'm old-fashioned."

"Them, anyway," said Marjorie undiverted. "They wouldn't touch it with a barge-pole because of the land being so tied up."

"I wasn't thinking of a mortgage," said Cynthia.

"What then?" demanded Marjorie. "Don't be so maddening, Cynthia."

Cynthia studied her finger-tips. "I was thinking of Jacqueline."

"And who's Jacqueline when she's at home?"

"Jacqueline, my dear, is Quentin Fent's intended or whatever you call it these days."

"And what about her?"

"She's the only daughter of Battersby's Bearings."

"What if she is?"

"Her father could finance any development you cared to mention," said Cynthia Paterson, "and from all that I've heard about him I don't think he's likely to be a preservationist either."

"Prunes?" echoed Detective Constable Crosby disbelievingly. He had taken Milly Pennyfeather to the cinema in Berebury, and was now giving her a drink in the saloon bar of The Crown and Anchor in Tollgate Street. "Black-coated workers, that's what my landlady calls them."

"Prunes," repeated Milly. "That's what I said. You're ever so interested in Sat'day night, aren't you?"

"I like to know how the other half lives, that's all," said Crosby, cradling his glass. He wished Milly had made her own drink last half as long. "Prunes with meat sounds right weird to me."

Milly wrinkled her nose. "I know. We only have them in our house for breakfast and then not always but people like that are funny. They were mixed with sausage meat."

"Cor," said Crosby. "You don't say."

"Stuffing," said Milly confidently. "Quite nice, really."

"You tasted it?"

"Well, just to see what it was like. No harm in that, is there?"

"What about the others? Did they like it?"

"Dunno," she said indifferently. "I didn't do no serving so I couldn't see if they all ate it up like good little children." She sighed. "Wasn't Sampson Ghent marvellous in the big picture? Those muscles on his chest . . ."

"The cold soup," said Crosby, "did you try that?"

Milly's lips contracted in an expression of distaste. "Couldn't bring myself to touch it."

"I should think not," agreed Crosby stoutly. "Why wasn't it hot?"

"Search me," said Milly. "Talking about hot, what did you think of Sampson Ghent in those swimming pool scenes?"

"Ah," said Crosby wisely, "that's not him in the pool. That's his stand-in."

"Never!"

"S'fact," said Crosby, who had taken an instant dislike at first sight to the great Sampson Ghent and every single one of his bulging muscles. "He doesn't go near the water himself. Spoil his make-up."

"You're just jealous." She eyed him appraisingly. "Though I daresay you got some muscles of your own inside that shirt. What was it you said you did?"

"Caretaker," said Crosby, buttoning his jacket.

She tossed her head. "Thought so. I said to Mum you're not in the building trade."

"I can carry as many bricks as . . ."

"It's not that. It's the money. They're always flush week-ends."

Crosby gave in and finished his drink. "Same again?"

"I don't mind if I do."

"They had a fancy pudding, too, didn't they?" said Crosby when he got back with the drinks. "Cheers."

"You can say that again. Cheers."

"Why?"

"Don't ask me," said Milly. "Mrs. Fent chose the menu. She didn't ask my advice."

"Can't think why not," said Crosby mendaciously. "Did you get any pudding?"

Milly shook her head regretfully. "There were only the twelve of them. One each. They were made special the day before."

"Ah . . ."

"Mrs. Fent had those six little dishes with holes in that she brought back from France last summer. Crémets or something, they were called. You fill them with cream and egg-white and put it in muslin."

"Muslin," said Crosby, genuinely surprised. "You're sure?"

"'Course I'm sure." She looked at him suspiciously. "Why? What do you want to know for?"

"I don't." He leaned forward. "I just want to take your mind off Sampson Ghent."

"Get away with you." Milly giggled. "You are a one."

"Come on then, concentrate on the pudding. You fill these little dishes with the creamy stuff and muslin . . ."

"You line the dish with the muslin, then you put the stuff in and leave it in a cold place to drain. Then you tip it out onto a plate, cover it with sugar and cream, and serve it with raspberries."

"There," he said triumphantly. "Now you've forgotten all about Sampson Ghent."

"No, I haven't," said Milly.

"And Mrs. Fent did this twice?"

"That's right. She had six dishes. That made twelve. One each. But she gave me some raspberries to take home to Mum because there wasn't one over for me. Then they went on to the cheese and port."

"What colour are his eyes?"

"Brown," said Milly promptly. "I'll tell you what I did try, though. The wine. Mrs. Fent didn't touch hers. Left it in the glass. So I had that while I was clearing away. Quite nice it was, too."

"Ghent's eyes were blue," said Crosby.

Milly poked his chest affectionately. "Brown. I'd never forget a thing like that. I've seen all his films." She put her glass down and looked into his eyes. "Do you remember that scene at the end when he was reunited with his childhood sweetheart? That wasn't no stand-in."

"It's high time you went home, young Milly," said Crosby.

NINE

Detective Inspector Sloan spent his evening on the case too.

At home.

"Margaret," he asked his wife, "how would you plan a dinner party for twelve?"

"I shouldn't," said Mrs. Margaret Sloan. "Why? You haven't asked a whole team here, have you?"

"No, but it's a thought." He grinned. "Just to prove how wrong they were."

"What about?"

"Bachelordom."

"Don't you dare. Besides, we haven't twelve of everything, have we?"

"No. But," persisted her spouse, "if you had to, what would you give them to eat?"

"Well, now," she sat back in the easy-chair, considering, "when everything's done and dusted you can't beat a roast for a real crowd."

"What about crown of lamb?"

"Good idea. It would be nice and cheap, too."

"Cheap?" That was something that hadn't occurred to Sloan.

"All you need are two joints of best end of lamb and that's not a dear cut. You'd get a good meal for twelve out of that for as little as anything else bar a stew."

"Would you now . . . I knew I'd married a good manager."

"I don't know if your mother would agree with you there."

"Ah, well . . . that's different."

"Yes." She eyed him as if she was about to say something more. "Perhaps it is. Anyway, crown of lamb makes a very nice-looking dish, too," she told him. "It looks more splendid than it is. You get the butcher to remove the chine bones and then you sew up both ends together back to back."

Sloan nodded comprehension. "Then you cook it."

"Then," she explained patiently, "you fill the ring in the centre with plenty of stuffing. And, of course, if you want to gild the lily . . ."

"Yes?" Anything could be a clue at this stage. Anything at all.

"Then you put cutlet frills on the ends of the bones."

"Cutlet fri . . . oh, I know. Those paper things that look like chef's hats for dolls." All he hoped was that he never had to try to explain them to Superintendent Leeyes, that was all.

Margaret Sloan smiled and a thrill of warm contentment went through him. "It's not too bad, being married to a policeman, is it?" he said.

"Not bad at all," she said in the faintly dry tone she used where someone else might have got emotional.

"Wait until I'm out every night in a row for a month."

"I'll go home to Mother . . ."

"Or I have to go after a mad gunman." He moved forward. "You'd better kiss me now in case I don't come back when I do."

"Idiot. Now about those frills . . ."

"It doesn't matter about the frills. A plain kiss will do."

"With the frills on the tips of the bones," she said firmly, "the circle really does look like a crown."

"I've often wondered what they were used for."

"Effect"—she frowned—"unless you're meant to pick them up at that end for a good chew."

"You can lose the best bit of a chop with only a knife and fork," pronounced Sloan judicially. "There's nothing like the fingers."

"Anyway, the frills make something special of it." She turned towards the bookcase. "I expect I can rustle up a picture of it for you. The cookery books usually do a photograph of one." She ran a finger along the bookshelf. "We had enough of them given to us for wedding presents. I don't know what everyone thought I was going to do— starve you. There's something else that you can do if the cook has an artistic frame of mind—had she?"

"I don't know," said Sloan. "I haven't seen enough of her to find out. Yet. All we know about her to date is that she's small, dark, and very attractive."

"But you didn't notice her particularly?"

"No," he said, straight-faced. "Only in the police sense."

"I know." She nodded. "Strictly in the line of duty. It's not too bad, being a policeman, is it?"

"You learn to notice things," said Margaret's husband. "Five foot four, I should say. Black hair . . ."

"So that you would know her again in a crowd?"

"Have to keep your eyes open on the job."

"Naturally."

"Good legs and better ankles."

"Which dish are we talking about now?"

Sloan grinned. "Crown of lamb. Why did you want to know if Mrs. Fent was artistic?"

"If she was, then she'd probably pipe creamed potatoes round the outside edge of the lamb."

"And that looks like ermine, I suppose."

"Idiot," she said for the second time.

"Especially with the odd pea strategically placed in the potato," he said.

"I'd better put the coffee on."

Later he came back to the subject of the meal at Strontfield Park.

"Perhaps, Margaret, you can tell me something else?"

"Yes, Officer?"

"Why would Mrs. Fent have served cold soup?"

"Less trouble than grapefruit," replied Mrs. Sloan without hesitation. "And cheaper than melon. And pâté—what your mother and mine used to make themselves and call potted meat—is out because you can't do hot toast for twelve if you've got the roast on your mind."

"But why was the soup served cold?"

"Because that meant she could dish it out earlier—before the guests arrived, perhaps. Serving twelve plates of hot soup from a tureen is a bit of a performance and even if you pour it out beforehand hot it'll be cold by the time you've got twelve people sitting down and settled. Cold soup's quite nice, anyway."

"Never." He took his coffee from the tray. "Aren't you having any?"

She shook her head. "It upset my tummy last night."

"Do you realize, Margaret, that we don't even know where the people were all sitting at that table and yet it's all China to a sixpence that one of them poisoned Bill Fent."

"Well," she responded promptly, "with those sort of people you can be sure that the chief lady guest would have been on the host's left and the chief gentleman ditto on the hostess's left, second most important on the host's right and hostess's right. That's six for you."

"So Fent would have had Mrs. Washby on his left—the whole show was in her honour—and," he cast his mind through the diners' names, "Miss Paterson, would you say, on his right? She was the oldest . . ."

"But unmarried," said Mrs. Sloan. "I'd say that the next oldest married woman would be there."

"Mrs. Ursula Renville. I must say I rather liked the look of her."

"Then," said Margaret Sloan ironically, "you may be sure that she'll have been next to the host."

"That would put Dr. Washby on one side of Mrs. Fent and Richard Renville on the other."

"With your Miss Paterson next to Dr. Washby and the next most important male . . ."

"The professor for sure . . ."

"Next to Mrs. Washby."

Sloan opened his notebook. "That only leaves the Marchmonts . . ."

"The next on each side . . ."

"And the two cousins, Annabel Pollock and Quentin Fent."

"Family," said Margaret immediately. "You can put them in anywhere."

"So," said Sloan slowly, "the cold soup would have been on the table and with a bit of luck anyone knowing the set-up and coming into the room beforehand would have worked out where nearly everyone was going to be asked to sit."

Mrs. Sloan shivered suddenly. "I hadn't thought of it that way."

"Especially the host and hostess—if you knew the head and foot of the table." He went back to his notebook. "After the soup the crown of lamb with its stuffing and its fancy potatoes and what else?"

She paused for thought. "At this time of the year beans and peas, I should think, and then new potatoes—oh, and red currant jelly."

"That's hardly letting the dog see the rabbit for trimmings," he objected.

"That," said the prudent housewife, "is the whole idea. It makes the rabbit go further."

He looked at the clock and shut his notebook. "I'll have to find out more about that pudding in the morning."

"She knew what she was doing, this Mrs. Fent of yours," observed his wife. "That's a clever meal to do for twelve."

"Clever?" That was something else he hadn't thought of either. That Mrs. Helen Fent was a clever woman was something that he conscientiously made a note of.

"Inexpensive, then," amended Margaret Sloan. "I shouldn't think you could do much for less." She gathered up his empty coffee cup. "Mostly prepared the day before, easy to serve and nice to look at without being ostentatious."

"Neat but not gaudy," agreed Sloan looking for the cat to put it out.

"Helen! Helen, what on earth are you doing down here? And at this time of night . . ."

Helen Fent started. "Oh, it's only you, Annabel. You gave me quite a fright."

"And you gave me quite a fright," countered the young nurse briskly. "I thought you were nicely tucked up in bed . . ."

"I was . . ."

"And then I find you pattering about downstairs in your night-dress. It's a white one, too."

Helen gave a shaky little laugh. "I expect I do look a bit like a ghost."

"In the dark as well." Annabel was reproachful. "You might have put a light on."

"Sorry," she said penitently. "I didn't think."

"I was just coming up to bed anyway," said Annabel. "I would have come in to see if you needed anything for the night. Did you want another hot drink?"

"Yes . . . no. No"—Helen took a deep breath—"thank you."

"Or a sleeping tablet? I've got some with me."

"No, thank you." Helen shook her head. "It's not that. I was just making quite sure we were all locked up for the night."

"We are tonight," said Annabel. "I must admit that we weren't last night. At least I found the garden door hadn't been locked when I went by last thing. I locked it myself. I meant to tell you but this morning there didn't seem time."

"No," agreed Helen gravely. "It's been quite a day."

"Quentin must have forgotten it."

Helen passed a hand in front of her eyes. "It was one of the things Bill always used to see to. It's not Quentin's fault—he's got enough to think about as it is—it's mine. I've just got to get used to doing things like that without Bill."

"Tonight," said Annabel Pollock not unkindly, "all you've got to get used to is staying in bed."

"Sorry, Nurse"—Helen smiled faintly in the darkness—"but that's not as easy as you might think."

"No," agreed Annabel sympathetically, "but better get back to bed now all the same. Call me if you want anything—and do try to get some sleep."

"Where's Quentin?"

"In the study. He's on the phone to Jacqueline. She rang ages ago and they're still at it."

For Quentin Fent the course of true love never had run smooth so it was no more choppy than usual as he tried to explain to Jacqueline Battersby that he was the new owner of Strontfield Park.

"Unless," he finished, "anything happens to me in the next three weeks."

"Does that mean that Daddy will let us get married now?" she asked with feminine directness. Not for nothing had her father made his money by calling a spade a spade.

"I hope so but"—Quentin was cautious—"it's a real barn of a place."

"Strontfield Park." She let the name roll around in her mind. "There have been Fents there for generations, haven't there?"

"Yes," said Quentin rather shortly, "and between them they've used up what money they ever had."

"Daddy says property's better than money."

"I daresay it is," rejoined her fiancé with spirit, "when you've got both. One without the other's a bit of a bind."

"All the same," said Mr. Battersby's daughter shrewdly, "Daddy will be pleased when he hears."

"He'll probably change his mind when he's seen the place," said Quentin pessimistically.

"Why? What's wrong with it?"

"Nothing. That's the trouble. Don't get the idea that it's not very nice. It is. Too nice. With every preservation order, entail, covenant, and God knows what slapped on it and"—for a moment Quentin forgot his devotion to the world of fine art—"you can't even alter a flipping window without asking the whole world."

"Didn't you once tell us something about some development or other?" Miss Battersby was every inch her father's daughter—and more.

"I did," said Quentin reluctantly. He thought it high time the conversation took a more romantic turn. "I shall have to go into all that now with the legal eagles, but in the meantime, my love . . ."

"Daddy'll want to know," said Jacqueline practically.

"Look here," exploded Quentin hotly, "am I marrying you or asking planning permission?"

"Both, I hope," said his affianced sweetly. "Together. When?"

"Name the day," snarled Quentin.

Miss Battersby drew breath. "Shall we say a month to-morrow?"

"Making sure, aren't you?" he said bitterly.

"If you're making an honest woman of me in a church," said Jacqueline, "there's something called banns which take three weeks."

"All right, all right," said Quentin. "A month—if I live that long."

"You might if you keep out of Daddy's way. He still hasn't got his car back from the repairer's."

Quentin winced. Usually he found Jacqueline's forthrightness a refreshing contrast to the ambiguity of the conversation in the London art circles in which he moved. Today it had all the double-edged quality of a drawn broadsword. He said, "Right. A month tomorrow, then."

"It's a date," her voice came over the telephone faintly mocking.

"And don't forget that you've said yes," he added crossly, "even if your precious father doesn't change his mind."

"He will now," she said, "don't worry about that. Now, listen, darling . . ."

The conversation between the engaged pair, business over, then got down to essentials and it was a good twenty minutes later when Quentin rang off and went to bed. He left Strontfield Park to darkness and the monotonous ticking of the Quare clock in the drawing-room.

This room was never entirely dark, never entirely quiet.

When all the other lights in the room had been extinguished for the night one always burned here. It was beside a bank of tiny flickering screens looking rather like a television shop-window which was showing the same programme on five different sets. Only an expert could have told that the five moving green and black outlines showed five different programmes.

And that expert was sitting in front of the screens watching carefully.

Her name was Nurse Joan Brown and this was the Intensive Care Unit of Berebury District General Hospital.

Each of the five green lines recorded the beats of one ailing heart, each of the green dots that ran across the bottom of the screens monitored a highly irregular pulse.

The noise—a susurration which never completely faded away—came from a ventilator. It was one of the mechanical aids with which the doctors were trying to keep Mr. Tom Exley alive. His wife, who was still by his bedside, didn't know by now whether she loved or hated its faint monotonous "suff-suff" sound which had become part of the background to her life since last Saturday night. One thing she had learned by now was that the delicate pink flush on her husband's cheeks owed everything to the machine and nothing to the healthy processes of natural life.

It was just after two o'clock in the morning when a new sound disturbed the little ward.

Nurse Brown looked up.

The monitor representing Mr. Exley's pulse had emitted a warning bleep. She reached for the telephone. Even as she did so the green dot on the monitor screen trailed disconsolately downward and disappeared.

Mrs. Tom Exley's vigil was over now.

Nurse Brown led her away.

TEN

Sloan had begun his day—the Saturday—over toward Calleford—in Lampard, to be exact.

The clerk to the Lampard Bench of Magistrates was called Phillipps. He expressed himself delighted to be of any assistance to the inspector.

"From one arm of the Law to another," he put it felicitously.

"Er—quite," said Sloan hastily before the clerk could go on to their being brothers under the skin which he didn't feel they were. Not with the clerk in pin-stripe trousers and black jacket anyway. "It's just a few inquiries about your Bench . . ."

"They're quite good," said Mr. Phillipps in the manner of a modest ringmaster. "Of course," he added as one professional to another, "like all lay people they're a bit wayward at times. There's one in particular that's a bit mettlesome . . ."

"A lady, I expect," said Sloan, who had had his fill of lady magistrates before being promoted to sergeant let alone inspector.

"She can be handled, of course." The ringmaster had been succeeded by the lion tamer.

"And a do-gooder into the bargain?" He still hadn't made up his mind whether or not they did the most harm.

The clerk nodded. "Can't see the wood for the trees and never will. But on the whole, justice is done."

"I'm glad to hear it," said Sloan. And he was.

"Of course," went on the clerk, paternal now, "they none of them sleep the night after they sentence a man to prison for the first time."

"No." It would be, thought Sloan, like making one's first arrest. Aloud he said, "Mr. William Fent . . ."

"A sad loss," intoned Mr. Phillipps at once. "The pick of the bunch, you might say. A good man and a good magistrate, too. He'd been chairman for the last couple of years, you know. Like his grandfather."

"Did he," asked Sloan, "sentence harshly?"

"Not him," said the clerk. "On the contrary, I should say, thanks to Mr. Wilkins."

"Mr. Wilkins?"

"He's the probation officer."

"Ah," said Sloan understanding immediately and putting the police point of view from force of habit. "We knock 'em off and he gets 'em off."

Mr. Phillipps straightened his tie. "He's—er—very persuasive, Inspector. Makes them bend over backward to help every time."

A lion tamer but a better lion tamer, in fact.

Sloan, who belonged to the school of thought which favoured bending over forward more often, merely said, "Much crime over your way?"

"Not crime exactly," said the clerk expansively, "but we're the back door of Society's stables and that's where you see the breeder's mistakes, isn't it?"

"The misfits," agreed Sloan, wondering just how much of a misfit you'd have to be to hand a man a dollop of poison and wait for him to die. Selfish, for a start, to need to do it anyway; conceited to think you could do it and get away with it; clever to do it and get as far as he had done; cruel not to care how and when a man died; calculating, to weigh the pros and cons, because if there was one thing which stood out like a sore thumb about this case it was that it was no eleventh hour job. There wasn't a single sign of blind panic or urgent fear anywhere about that careful dose of soluble barbiturate in crowded company . . .

"Sorry," apologized Sloan, coming to with a jerk. "I didn't quite catch that . . ."

"Mostly motoring and matrimonial these days," repeated the clerk regretfully. "A drunk or two. Nothing exciting."

"Wine, women, and cars," said Sloan, considering how the persuasive Mr. Wilkins would account for the man who had tried to murder William Fent, justice of the peace. There was no telling of course—perhaps his mother had formed an alliance with a carpet-bag, perhaps he'd seen something nasty in the woodshed, perhaps he'd been born crippled—psychologically crippled, that is, or perhaps it was only because his dad hadn't lammed the difference between right and wrong into him the very first time he'd strayed over that invisible line . . .

"A bit of poaching, of course," continued the clerk. "Always a bit of that in the country."

"Since Shakespeare and before," agreed Sloan. "Was he hard on it?"

"Not particularly." The clerk shook his head. "You can't do a lot with gypsies, you know."

"Not even Mr. Wilkins?"

Mr. Phillipps acknowledged this with a quick smile. "Not even Mr. Wilkins. They pay their fines and go and do it again. Almost instead of paying rates and taxes, you might say."

" 'The lesser breeds without the Law' and all that," murmured Sloan absently, his mind elsewhere. Come to think of it, law was a privilege, whatever the convicted said. "It's hardly a Newgate Calendar, is it?" He frowned. "Was there anything he did come down on, your Mr. Fent?"

"Guns," responded the clerk without hesitation. "Fire-arms certificates and so forth. Everyone's a bit nervous about fire-arms these days."

Sloan was glad to hear it. He himself was nervous about fire-arms all the time. Especially in the line of duty. The firing line, you might say.

"Was there," he carried on patiently with his questions, "anyone whom he had it in for in a big way?"

"Mr. Fent? Oh, no, Inspector. He wasn't that sort of man. He would never have taken advantage of his position like that, and he wouldn't have let anyone else on the Bench either, and neither would I."

"Male or female?" suggested Sloan slyly.

"Male or female," said Mr. Phillipps with emphasis.

"Well," said Sloan doggedly, "could there have been anyone gunning for him?"

Mr. Phillipps looked puzzled. "Someone he'd sentenced, you mean?"

"People do bear grudges," said Sloan, "especially those people who have been sentenced against those people who sentence them."

Mr. Phillipps' brow cleared. "There's no one that I can call to mind, Inspector."

"What about some boys called Pennyfeather?"

"Not them," said the clerk emphatically. "Always very friendly, not to say comic."

"Laughter in court?" suggested Sloan.

"Frequently. Always plenty to say for themselves. The press love it. They have a field-day when the Pennyfeathers come up."

"And not in love with their rocking-horses?"

"Definitely not. Cheerful lads. No ill will there."

"I wonder," said Sloan thoughtfully, "which end of their jelly babies they ate first."

Mr. Phillipps started. "Pardon, Inspector?"

"There was a psychiatrist we had once over in Berebury who always wanted to know."

Mr. Phillipps subsided. "The Pennyfeather brothers are all quite normal, anyway. There are four of them—like a blessed row of Toby jugs. They'll be all right when they grow up. They lead each other on, of course, and they've got quite a following among the smaller fry. That always makes them worse, you know."

Sloan did know. It was the first thing that they taught young constables—that most offences were committed by young males in groups. He didn't know why they bothered. It was something the man on the beat found out for himself on his first day in uniform.

Mr. Phillipps added the ultimate accolade to the family: "Never ask for time to pay either."

Sloan dismissed the Pennyfeather brothers from his mind—and the case. Somehow, cheerful acceptance of rough justice didn't accord with murder. He tried another tack with the magistrate's clerk. "What about in the past?"

"Back a bit, you mean?" He looked at Sloan curiously.

"I mean," he said, "someone who might have gone in some time ago but who might have come out recently with an outsize chip on his shoulder."

"I see what you're getting at now, Inspector." The clerk looked suddenly grave. "I can't call anyone to mind at all but I'll go through my records straightaway."

Detective Constable William Edward Crosby, English right down to his last entrenched Anglo-Saxon attitude, stepped inside the Post Office in the Calleshire village of Cullingoak, walked up to the counter, pulled out his warrant card and said out of the corner of his mouth in the best precinct-style the one word "Police."

He always announced himself this way when he was out on duty alone. As wiser men have discovered, there is a Walter Mitty in us all, and Constable Crosby's secret life had transatlantic overtones. Kill the fantasy, though, and something in the man dies too. (Crosby hadn't yet discovered that it is one of life's little ironies that when the fantasy comes true it is so like something happening to someone else as to be barely credible.)

In this instance the reaction of the postmistress, Mrs. MacArthur, brought Crosby down to earth with a bump.

"'Bout time, too," she snapped, continuing to assault a parcel with a date-stamp. "Here you are, Jim." She turned and tossed the parcel through a doorway to someone at the back. Having thus made it clear that—in her canon—policemen were small beer compared with postmen, she turned back to Crosby and demanded, "When are they going to do something about my kiosk—that's what I want to know. I've been on to them until I'm blue in the face."

Crosby took a breath.

Mrs. MacArthur didn't. "And they say that as fast as they put telephones in, the vandals rip them out, and do you ever catch 'em? Never! Now, you mark my words, young man . . ."

There was nothing in the world that annoyed Crosby more than to be called a young man, because he was and it showed. Walter Mitty hadn't been young, either.

". . . one of these days someone is going to want you people in a hurry"—even in full verbal flood Mrs. MacArthur contrived to sound as if she found this hard to believe—"and then what'll happen? You won't come and we'll all be murdered in our beds, that's what."

It was Crosby's private opinion that whoever murdered Mrs. MacArthur would be doing humanity—if not Her Majesty's Mails—a service, but all he said was "I'm making inquiries, madam, that's all."

Mrs. MacArthur hit another parcel with quick ferocity. "If it's about the license for the dog that bit the vicar, they've got one. Seventh-day Adventists, they are, too, though they got the vet for the dog quick enough."

"It's about last Saturday night," said Crosby with dignity, giving religious dogma a wide berth.

"Saturday nights there's always trouble." Mrs. MacArthur peered out of the Post Office window. In fact the village of Cullingoak presented an idyllic view to the world, from the church right down to the regulation patch of green, duck-pond and ducks, but Mrs. MacArthur was not deceived. "If it's not the pub it's the village hall. It's my belief that men only play cricket for the beer . . ."

"Not that sort of trouble."

"There was a dance at the Youth Club." She gave a merry cackle. "There's a different sort of trouble for you, if you like."

"Someone taken ill," said Crosby.

"Ah."

"The doctor knocked you up."

"What if he did?"

"Why?"

"Looking for someone ill in Copway Street, he said he was, and couldn't find them." She cocked her head to one side and said shrewishly, "Doctor in trouble then?"

Crosby shook his head. "Just a routine inquiry, madam."

"I know your sort of inquiries," she snorted. "Like the Spanish Inquisition. Someone always ends up in trouble."

"What time was this?"

"'Bout half past eleven. Party taken ill by the name of Waters, he said, but he couldn't place them. And he couldn't find them either. Not in Copway Street."

"And you?"

"I couldn't call the name to mind myself," she admitted. "Not then. 'Course we don't sort the letters here any more. Then I would have known. And the telephone exchange has gone automatic, too."

Crosby shuddered gently at the thought of Mrs. MacArthur monitoring either, let alone both. "So you never did find . . ."

"Not then," she repeated. "Afterwards I remembered the people in Rose Cottage. Waters is their name."

"Waters, Rose Cottage, Copway Street." He wrote it down.

"Artists," she said succinctly. "Only here at the weekends. That's why the doctor didn't know the name. Seems as if the husband had an attack of asthma earlyish in the evening, then he got worse suddenly and as the doctor hadn't come she popped him in the car and drove him straight to the hospital in Berebury."

"So when the doctor did come the house was all locked up and empty," Crosby finished for her.

"That's right. He said he tried Rose Cottage and there was no one there." Mrs. MacArthur looked at him sideways. "The doctor had a woman in his car with him."

"His wife," said Crosby.

Mrs. MacArthur sniffed and changed her tune smartly. "I'm glad to hear it, I'm sure. A doctor should be married, shouldn't he?"

"We all need wives," said Crosby, wondering about Mr. MacArthur.

She leered at him. "That wasn't what I meant at all, young man, and well you know it."

There couldn't really have ever been any connection between Crosby and the Spanish Inquisition. Torquemada would never have blushed.

It was Police Inspector Harpe who gave Sloan the news about Tom Exley's death when he got to Berebury. He seemed to Sloan to be taking a regrettably parochial view of it, too. Perhaps you could get too specialized, even in the police force.

"You must admit, Sloan, that it makes a nice point."

"What does?" asked Sloan, who could think of nothing nice about it at all.

"Whether I count him or you do."

Sloan looked blank. "Come off it, Harry . . ."

"What I mean is," said the Traffic man, "is he mine or is he yours?"

"He's dead," responded Sloan with vigour. "That's all anyone's told me so far."

"Statistically," explained Harpe, "I mean is he one of yours or one of mine. That's what I want to know."

"Oh, I see . . ." Sloan opened his mouth and shut it

again. He might as well save his breath. It was no use telling Happy Harry that statistics had never made any
difference to anything he'd ever met so far. The good ones
just told you what you should have known anyway: stating
the obvious with figures to prove it. As for the bad ones
. . .

"Is this man Exley a Road Traffic Accident death," elaborated Happy Harry still further, "or . . ."

"Ah, yes, I see . . ." Sloan should have remembered that
Harpe was a born hair-splitter.

"Or is he a murder victim?" finished Happy Harry.

"He died from injuries received out of the use of a motor
vehicle on a public road," said Sloan solemnly. Two could
play at this game. "On the other hand . . ."

"Yes?"

"So did the other chap."

"No, no," said Harpe immediately. "You can have Fent.
He's yours. All yours."

"Thank you."

"Not at all," said Harpe, upon whom sarcasm in any
shape or form was completely wasted. "Someone tried to
murder Fent and he died. But Exley's different."

"I don't see why."

"Insurance," said Harpe. "Nobody had given him any
poison that we know of, but the insurance companies are
bound to argue that . . ."

"Watch them try to eel out of both," said Sloan bru-
tally, "and don't you go and make it any easier for them."

"The small print," began Harpe gloomily, "I expect that
. . ."

Sloan sighed. He wasn't a small print man himself.
Never had been. Nor if it came to that was he very interested in things which were legal without being honest. His
mother—that was where you learned these things, at your
mother's knee—had brought him up on a much stricter cri-
terion than mere legality.

"Exley," he said categorically, "is as clear a case of misadventure as I've ever come across whatever anyone says."

"It's not really a verdict any longer"—Harpe always took the niggardly view—"not if the Crown can help it."

"Then it should be," said Sloan. "And, Harry . . ."

"Yes?"

"Don't forget, will you, that statistically most male murderers are widowers."

"Bah!" said the Traffic man.

Crosby met Sloan in the corridor outside the Traffic Department's room, a flimsy message sheet in his hand.

"News, Crosby,"

"From Australia. A proper turn up for the book, sir, if you ask me," said the constable handing the paper over. "Quick, too."

"They do it with boomerangs." Sloan took it and began to read. Swifter than Ariel the police telex system had encircled the earth and come back with that most precious police commodity—information. Somewhere in an antipodean land—Cunningham's Gap, Queensland, to be exact—a fellow copper had plodded about making an inquiry for another policeman whom he had never seen and whose name he would never even know.

Standing in the corridor in Berebury, Calleshire, England—oh, ever so England—Sloan tried to visualize the man making his way through a dry and dusty township, though for all he knew Cunningham's Gap could be in the middle of tropical rain forest and his fellow copper a lady policewoman. He looked at the message again.

An Englishman called Hector Fent, subject of inquiry, had died of natural causes at an address in Cunningham's Gap nearly five years ago . . .

This was news to Sloan. That didn't matter. What mattered was if it was news to a certain murderer. Or did he know?

Said to be a widower, ran on the message cautiously.

That could mean anything or nothing.

One son, continued the telex.

Which could mean a lot.

Name of Peter Miller Fent spelled out the capitals.

Which did mean a lot.

Quite a lot.

ELEVEN

All inquiries set in train—especially of Government departments—tend to produce results.

In time.

Unfortunately Sloan was not in the Police Station at Berebury when Dr. Writtle rang, and the analyst, mistaking rank for knowledge, had misguidedly spoken with Superintendent Leeyes instead.

"This query of yours to the Home Office, Sloan," said Leeyes, when the detective inspector did appear in his office, "about the manufacture of soluble barbiturates . . ."

"Sir?"

"Barbiturates," Leeyes informed him, "are derived from barbituric acid or malonyl urea."

Sloan got out his notebook.

"And malonyl urea"—the superintendent spoke as one to whom organic chemistry was an open book—"is prepared by the condensation of di . . . di . . . diethyl"—the impression of expertise faded at the third attempt—"that's it . . . diethyl ester of malonic acid with urea."

"Really, sir? Thank you, sir."

"The barbiturates are prepared by the addition to the parent compound of various chemical groups," growled Leeyes. "Blinding us with science, Sloan, that's what they're trying to do."

"Yes, sir."

"This technical stuff," carried on Leeyes, cutting one of the country's most highly qualified analytical chemists down to size in passing, "is all very well in its way, but it doesn't help to solve the case, does it?"

"Too soon to say, sir. Did he mention the taste?"

Leeyes pushed some papers about. "I've got that here somewhere. The taste . . . oh, yes. Not nice."

"How noticeable?"

"It would need to be disguised a bit. Or so he said." The superintendent discounted all expert opinion on principle.

"And the—er—natural sources of this barbiturate?"

"Malonyl urea?" said Leeyes airily. "Writtle went on a bit about that. Malic acid—that's where you start from—comes in three optically isometric forms."

"Does it?" responded Sloan sourly. "Any of them home-grown?"

"Yes."

Sloan looked up sharply.

"Apples," said Leeyes, "grapes, beet-root—oh, and rhubarb."

"Rhubarb?"

"That's what he said. I suppose he knows."

"What about this business of making it at home?"

"He wouldn't say yes and he wouldn't say no."

Sloan said something very decisive indeed.

"He did say you'd need to have the know-how and the equipment," said Leeyes, "and something called ethylene dichloride. He's putting it all in writing for you."

For once Sloan didn't think this would help. "I think we'll have to go back to square one, sir," he sighed, "and find out who gains."

"Or even who doesn't lose," said Leeyes pessimistically.

"Exley's lost for a start," said Sloan, and told him about the other driver. "Poor chap."

Leeyes drummed his fingers on his desk. "And we're no further forward, are we, Sloan?"

"We know someone gave Fent poison . . ."

"We knew that on Monday," said Leeyes.

"And which poison," said Sloan, tapping his notebook.

"Academic," said Leeyes inexorably.

"And who had the opportunity."

"Too many." The superintendent's response was prompt and gloomy. "Much too many. Eleven, at least."

Sloan cleared his throat. "Thirteen, actually . . ."

"Unlucky for some." Leeyes's reaction to the number thirteen was culled from the Bingo hall.

". . . if we include Peter Miller from the farm next door to Strontfield," Sloan told him why, "and that girl Milly Pennyfeather slaving over a hot stove in the kitchen."

"Let's," said Leeyes dourly. "The more the merrier."

"As I see it," Sloan pressed on regardless, "any of them could have nipped into the dining-room with the goods and done their damnedest."

"There's no need to be melodramatic about it," said the superintendent tetchily.

"No, sir." Sloan took a breath, thought about his pension, and let it out again. "What I meant is that Milly just showed them the room for their coats and then dashed back to the kitchen. She left them to find their own way to the drawing-room."

"And you think one of them went via the dining-room?"

"Could be, sir. They all knew the house well. Except for Mrs. Washby."

Leeyes started tapping his fingers on the desk again. "What else do we know? Apart from this chap next door having a finger in the pie."

Sloan coughed. "I hear the widow's behaving a bit oddly."

"Widows do," said Leeyes with deep feeling.

"She didn't like us being at the funeral. And now she's shut herself up in her room and won't see anyone at all—let alone us."

Leeyes sighed. "Sloan, you've been in the Force long enough to know that nobody likes us being anywhere. Unless somebody goes for them, of course. Then it's different."

"Yes, sir." It was easiest to agree with him. Always.

"Anything else?"

"Who know who gains," advanced Sloan cautiously. "Some of them, anyway."

"Who?"

"Quentin Fent for one. A lot. And through him, his fiancée. Jacqueline Battersby."

"Not . . ."

"Yes. None other. Old Battersby's daughter. From Luston."

"There are no better bearings than Battersby's," said Leeyes, proving that at least one advertising copy writer earned his daily bread. "She won't want for a penny or two. Anyone else?"

"Annabel Pollock. That's the other cousin. She only gains a little. Probably not enough to count, saving Eliza Doolittle."

"Saving who, Sloan?"

" 'My Fair Lady,' sir." Now his wife had really enjoyed that. He quoted: " 'Them as she lives with would have done her in for a hat pin let alone a hat.' "

"And who else," growled Leeyes, pointedly ignoring this, "gains?"

"The widow gets a life interest in not very much," replied Sloan.

Leeyes sniffed.

"And," went on Sloan carefully, "Peter Miller Fent— that is Hector Fent's branch of the family—stands a bit nearer than he did to whatever's going. Next in line after our Quentin, in fact."

"To the left, one pace, quick marrrrrrrch," drawled Leeyes sardonically. "That the lot?"

"We don't know about those who had something to lose," went on Sloan methodically, "but I should say that somebody somewhere still stands to make something out of planning permission in a big way."

The superintendent gave another elaborate sigh. "It isn't even as if we hadn't got anything else to do." He waved an arm toward the map on the wall behind him. It was a pointillist affair showing crime in Calleshire. "There's been another raid on the Hollandbury quarries."

"Again, sir? That's the third this year."

"That's right," agreed Leeyes. "Three months' supply for every safe-breaker in the county and then some. By my reaching their last lot'll be just about used up by now."

"I'm afraid Bertie's on the go again, too, sir," said Sloan, falling in with the change of subject. That would be another pin for the map. Or two, perhaps.

Leeyes grunted. "I thought he said he was going straight."

"That man," said Sloan, "would say anything except his prayers. They'll have to screw him into his grave when the time comes."

"It can't come soon enough for me, but there's worse trouble than Bertie about." Leeyes pointed to a cluster of pins on the outskirts of Berebury. "We've got a child molester on the new estate."

Sloan winced.

"I know, I know," said Leeyes. "It's their clothes, you know."

"Pardon, sir?"

"The kids. So nicely got up these days it's just putting them in temptation's way. We never had this trouble in the old days. Who'd want to entice a scruffy urchin with a runny nose and dirty old clothes and fleas . . ."

Only Superintendent Leeyes could have conjured up a picture of Dickensian squalor and presented it as a good.

"No one," finished Leeyes, thus writing off the efforts of several generations of social reformers as a bad thing.

"Go tell that to the sociologists," sang Sloan, but under his breath.

Dr. Harriet Baird stomped up the stairs to Helen Fent's bedroom in Strontfield Park. "Morning, m'dear," she said. "And what sort of a night have you had?"

"Not too bad," lied Helen.

The doctor felt her pulse. "That's more like it."

"I want to get up," said Helen.

"I daresay you do," said Dr. Baird calmly, noting the dark rings of sleeplessness under her patient's eyes, "but you aren't going to. Not today. Tomorrow, perhaps, if you're sensible. We'll see. Things sort themselves out all right downstairs yesterday?"

"I think so."

"Takes time," said the doctor wisely. "I should let it all flow over you for a bit. No hurry about anything, is there?"

"Not really, I suppose," admitted Helen in lifeless tones. "Not now. Not any more."

The doctor didn't argue about this. Instead she said, "And Annabel's looking after you all right, I'm sure."

"Between them," said Helen Fent to the doctor in a sudden burst of savagery, "Quentin and Annabel are managing everything very nicely, thank you."

There was a small dark-haired man waiting for Sloan in his office. Detective Constable Crosby performed the honours.

"This is Mr. Hickory, sir. The expert on Town and Country Planning you wanted to see."

"From the county architect's department at Calleford," added Mr. Hickory cautiously. "What can we do for you, Inspector?"

"You can explain to me," said Sloan, "about planning permission and development . . ."

Mr. Hickory drew breath.

Sloan added a hasty rider: ". . . in words that I can understand."

"I see. Well, planning permission's a funny thing . . ."

Sloan's eyebrows went up.

"No, no, Inspector. Don't misunderstand me. Not funny in the police sense, though you do get a bit of that, too, from time to time." Hickory smiled thinly. "I daresay we've all been approached in our day."

Sloan preserved a decent reticence on this. It wasn't the sort of thing policemen talked about among strangers.

"No, not funny," went on the planning man. "Quixotic would be a better word. Not in theory, mark you. Oh, dear, no. In thoery the surveyors recommend and the committees decide . . ."

"Man proposes, God disposes," muttered Crosby under his breath.

"And in theory," said Hickory, "the committees take all decisions in the best interests of the community as a whole . . ."

"Don't we all," said Sloan politely. Crosby just rolled his eyes.

"Yes—well," Hickory went on, "committees are funny things, too."

Sloan, who had made this discovery while still a constable, brought Mr. Hickory from the general to the particular: "About development at Strontfield Park . . ."

"Ah, yes." The local authority man unrolled a map of East Calleshire and pointed. "Here's Constance Parva. You see this part marked in yellow . . ."

Crosby craned his neck over Hickory's shoulder while Sloan examined the map for yellow markings.

"That's what's called the village envelope. Since the 1947 Town and Country Planning Act. Development is normally allowed within this area—except sometimes what we call backland housing. Outside it . . ."

"The white part?"

"That's right, Inspector. Permission for development of the white part is a bit different. Not so . . ."

"Automatic?"

"More debatable, shall we say," murmured Hickory. "Discretionary, in fact."

"And this main drainage they all talk about?"

"Drains," said Mr. Hickory delicately, "er—open the way for more development."

Crosby opened his mouth to speak.

"I can see that," said Sloan hurrying into the breach.

"They like churches, too," volunteered Hickory.

"Do they indeed!" said Sloan, suppressing a variety of retorts which included references to temples of Midas . . .

"They give the community a focal point," continued Hickory unabashed.

. . . and bowing in the house of Mammon. (Sloan's mother had been a great Bible reader.)

Hickory waved a hand. "From the Town and Country Planning point of view, I mean."

. . . to say nothing of worshipping at the altar of Moloch.

"So," managed Sloan sardonically, "given drains and a church . . ."

"In that order," mouthed Crosby, *sotto voce.*

". . . within the yellow village envelope you get development?"

"We'd rather," Hickory entered a caveat, "it wasn't first-class agricultural land."

"It isn't. Not at Strontfield," said Sloan.

Crosby looked surprised.

"If it was good enough to farm well," explained Sloan patiently, "Fent would have farmed it well and the farm next door wouldn't have got the name of Fallow."

"That's right." Mr. Hickory blinked and consulted some more papers. "That's what the applicants said. It's not productive land out there. They thought an injection of new blood would revitalize the rural community . . ."

"Very public-spirited of them, I'm sure," murmured Sloan.

"New houses would improve the shops and services," read out Hickory, "stop the drain from the countryside, and so forth . . ."

"They were in it for their health, then, I take it," said Sloan.

Mr. Hickory permitted himself a thin smile. "Not entirely."

"For sticky shovels, more like," said Crosby.

"It didn't even go to appeal," said Hickory. "They got outline permission on the first application so they must have been on a good wicket."

"Outline permission?"

Hickory twisted in his chair. "Taking the temperature of the water, you could call that. Agreed in principle, but you've still got to get the detail approved. And if you don't get outline . . ."

"Yes?" asked Sloan curiously.

". . . then you haven't had to go to the expense of designing the development you had in mind down to the last brick."

"But they got outline for Strontfield," said Sloan.

Hickory nodded. "Without a struggle."

"When?"

"July last year."

"Then what?"

"Then nothing. No detailed plans were ever submitted by the applicants."

"And who were they?"

"Calleford Enterprises Limited." Hickory flicked a paper over. "A couple of builders, a pair of local businessmen, the duke's cousin . . ."

"Ah, the lord on the board?"

"That's him." Mr. Hickory paused. "They say he's all right when he's sober."

"We do know him," remarked Sloan distantly. "Our Traffic people . . ."

"Quite so," said Mr. Hickory.

"They're always after his blood," revealed Crosby chattily. "Trouble is, he's so used to the stuff."

Sloan tried to get back to the land. "This outline permission . . ."

"They'll get him one day," said Crosby. "Inspector Harpe says that if it's the last . . ."

Sloan overrode Crosby. "Fent had no part in this application then?"

Hickory shook his head. "None. The owner's consent isn't necessary, but he is advised of both the application and the outcome."

"Seems fair enough," said the police officer.

"Usen't to be," said the planning man, "in the days before they notified the owner. He'd've sold his land to the developers before he woke up to what it was worth with permission. You'd be surprised . . ."

Sloan had stopped being surprised at the limitless nature of human folly and greed a long time ago. He said, "So what we've got here is some not too good agricultural land with outline planning permission for development for houses . . ."

"And a small shopping precinct."

"Which hasn't been taken up by the developers or anyone else," said Sloan, wondering how Peter Miller Fent and Fallow Farm fitted into this picture.

"To date," said Hickory.

"All of which," added Sloan to Crosby when the local authority man had gone, "may have everything or nothing at all to do with the death of William Fent."

"This might, though, sir." Crosby had picked up the

papers which Hickory had left with them. "Here, sir, take a look at this."

He handed over a sheet of business writing paper. It was headed "Calleford Enterprises Limited." In the list of directors was the name of R. Renville.

TWELVE

"Well," said Crosby eloquently, "do we have to throw a six or can we start now?"

"Now," said Sloan, getting to his feet.

"With Mr. Peter Miller Fent?"

"No. He'll keep for a bit."

"Renville?"

"No," said Sloan thoughtfully. "I think we'll start with the gardener woman. I bet she's the best talker of the lot of them."

Miss Cynthia Paterson's cottage in Constance Parva was at the church end of the High Street. It was quite small with a long sloping cat-slide roof at the back, and no front garden to speak of. They found the entrance at the side. They were led to it by a little notice set in the front wall over an arrow:

> Rich or poor
> Just the one door.

Sloan knocked on it. A dog barked somewhere but there was no answer.

"I can see an old bird in the greenhouse," remarked Crosby, peering about him.

The two policemen made their way across the garden to the greenhouse where a grey head was bobbing about amid the greenery.

"Won't keep you a moment," she called out through the door. "Come in. I'm just trying to catch a bee. There it is . . ."

Constable Crosby ducked hastily as something zoomed past his left ear.

"I don't know how it got in here," she said. "I do try not to let them get at the flowers."

The bee came back past Crosby. It sounded cross.

"Drat the thing," exclaimed Miss Paterson. "Look, there it is. Catch it, young man . . . it's not good for the flowers. Fast-moving insects are always dangerous to the garden. Some of the slow-moving ones aren't exactly helpful either."

Crosby picked up an empty flower-pot and advanced toward the bee. The bee retreated just out of his reach.

"The flowers do go off dreadfully if they're pollinated," lamented Miss Paterson, "and these are for show."

"Very nice they are, too," said Sloan politely.

"They won't be if that bee gets at them," said the lady gardener. "There it is—you'll get it now."

Unbidden, a snatch of his school-days came back to Sloan: a boyish Ariel helping a thicker-set Prospero into his cloak and singing, "Where the bee sucks, there suck I." The anxiety then, as he remembered it, had been to do with Ariel's voice breaking.

"I've often wondered how Buddhist gardeners get on," remarked Miss Paterson conversationally.

"Buddhists?" inquired Sloan.

"They're not allowed to kill anything—not even white fly."

The bee seemed unwilling to be killed either and sailed effortlessly upward and out of Crosby's reach.

"There's a chair," suggested Miss Paterson.

Crosby eyed a rickety example of bent woodwork, long superannuated from the kitchen, and said, "I think I can get it when it next comes down."

"Yes—you're tall enough." She swung round and glanced sharply at Sloan. "You're tall too. Policemen?"

"Yes, madam," said Sloan, and introduced themselves.

Miss Paterson nodded toward Crosby, and said, "He should be able to catch a bee, then, shouldn't he?"

"He should,"agreed Sloan cautiously, though there were moments when he doubted Crosby's capacity to catch anything.

It was hot in the greenhouse and the constable was perspiring gently now. The bee had speeded up.

"I've seen you both before, haven't I?" Miss Paterson adjusted her glasses and peered at the two police officers, "Yesterday. You were at Bill Fent's funeral. At the back of the church."

"Yes." Sloan hesitated and then told her about Tom Exley dying too. "We wanted to talk to you about the dinner party at Strontfield. Had anything been said that might have distracted Mr. Fent's concentration and so forth . . ."

Miss Paterson gave him a shrewd look. "There were no arguments, if that's what you mean, and he hadn't had too much to drink, either."

"The conversation?"

"Pretty general. At my end of the table anyway."

"You were between . . . ?"

"Dr. Washby and young Quentin Fent." She snorted delicately. "Anyone would think a country dinner party was a fertility rite—all the fuss Helen went to to get her table right as she called it." She tucked a wayward strand of grey hair into place, and said, "Everyone was being kind to the new girl—Dr. Washby's wife, that is. Veronica. She didn't really know any of us, so there wasn't too much local talk—not to begin with, anyway. After a bit, of course, you can't keep away from village chat—if you live in a village, that is. You know how it is."

"Any particular chat?" inquired Sloan casually.

He knew how it was, all right. That was one of the

things about the job. Once you were on it you could hardly talk about anything else. Not while you were at the police station anyway and half the time when you weren't either . . .

"Oh, just the usual . . ."

Crosby still hadn't caught the bee.

Miss Paterson waved a hand. "A post mortem on the village fête—that's always good for a bit of in-fighting—the Government—always something to talk about there . . ."

"Quite so," said Sloan with the strict impartiality demanded of the Best Police Force in the World.

"And the Pennyfeather brothers," recollected Miss Paterson. "They're our local bother boys. Somebody's usually got a story about them. Always on the look-out for trouble and finding it. Knock a man down as soon as look at him."

"Do you hear that, Crosby?" said Sloan. "You'll have to watch your step."

"Yes, sir." Crosby sounded glum. The bee—still at large —sounded outraged.

Miss Paterson forged on. "Yet another baby at Fallow Farm Cottage—they'll soon have to sleep head to tail down there—oh, and Gregory Fitch's father."

"What had he been up to?"

"Nothing. It's just that they managed to get him into an old folks' home at last, and Bill was telling us about it. Fitch'd been the Fents' gardener all his life—lived down in Keeper's Cottage beyond the old Folly but he'd reverted to stock a bit lately . . ."

Sloan, who grew roses for a hobby, nodded.

"Quite gone to seed," said Cynthia Paterson briskly. "Started talking nonsense about goings-on in the Folly and so on. Nature taking over again and all that. Civilization's not really very deep, is it?"

"Thin as paint," said the policeman feelingly. "Ask any man on the strength . . ."

"Anyway, in the end Paul Washby had to get him taken

away. Well, they'd tidied the old chap up so much over at the hospital that Greg didn't know him on the Sunday when he went in to see him. He told Bill he walked right past the end of the bed. Never seen him with his teeth in before, he said."

"Ah," said Sloan, who was of an age now to be sympathetic about teeth. He was peering out of the greenhouse while she spoke to see if he could spot signs of the cultivation of rhubarb.

"Mind you," said Miss Paterson showing an exemplary staying power with the original question, "being a mere woman I don't know what the gentlemen talked about when we left them."

"You left them?"

"All alone," she said solemnly, echoing his tone.

"All the men?" This added a new dimension to his inquiries about poisoning. "Why?"

"I shouldn't be surprised if it wasn't St. Paul," said the old rector's daughter unexpectedly. "Someone who didn't like women must have started it, mustn't they? And he didn't like women, I mean. St. Paul."

"Started what?" asked Sloan wildly.

"The custom. We're pretty backward out this way and we still leave 'em to it."

"Leave who to what, Miss Paterson?" The Mad Hatter's Tea Party sounded saner than this.

"The gentlemen to the port," she said, splashing some water on a potted salpiglossis. "This is a good colour, isn't it?"

"Oh, the port . . ." Sloan rapidly tried to call to mind what he knew about port. It wasn't a lot. You had to pass it to the left or something—that was it. Left was the port side. The opposite of starboard. There was another thing he'd heard about port.

"Tawny?" he said tentatively.

"Vintage, I should think," said Miss Paterson. "There."

"Just so," said Sloan. On quite another plane from life at Strontfield Park there was Kitty, Kitty. She was a disreputable old soak down in the town at Berebury, who had never been known to touch anything but port and lemon. She always came when she was called, did Kitty, Kitty . . . Now there was somebody who must know all there was to know about port.

"But as to what they talked about while they were sipping it, Inspector, I couldn't begin to say."

"I can see," said Sloan ponderously, "that Women's Lib hasn't got very far in Constance Parva."

Miss Paterson smiled thinly. "Too true. I only hope that Mrs. Washby isn't going to mind the change from London. The depths of the countryside aren't everyone's cup of tea."

"The village might grow," ventured Sloan.

He found a pair of alarmingly intelligent eyes fixed upon him. "Oh, you've heard about the new development, have you? Well, Inspector, that was one thing we didn't talk about—both sides being represented so to speak."

"Very wise, madam."

"And now it's not Bill's problem any more."

"No." Sloan cleared his throat. "Have you been up to the Park since—er—since . . ."

"No," she said gruffly. "Nothing I could say, is there? Or do. The doctor will have given her something—not that I've any time for doctors myself. Don't trust all these things they give you these days. Besides, only your contemporaries can give you comfort. Haven't you discovered that yet, Inspector? The young can't imagine how you feel. The oldies—like me—have got over it all long ago. Peer groups or some such nonsense they call it now." Abruptly Miss Paterson stooped down toward a cucumber plant and pinched something near the centre. "Always nip out the male flowers," she said, "if you want good cucumbers."

"Doesn't do anything for the bitterness, though," murmured the gardener within the policeman, the philosopher within the man. His gaze drifted from the cucumbers to the bee. "You only want to find a bird to chat with now, Crosby," he said pleasantly, "and then you'll know the lot."

"Yes, sir, I—" The constable didn't finish the sentence. There was a sudden commotion near the door of the greenhouse, and Crosby shot outside into the open air, hotly pursued by an exceedingly irate bee.

"That," observed Miss Paterson dryly, "seems to have done the trick. Thank you, Constable."

"Died? Mr. Exley?" exclaimed Ursula Renville. "Oh, I am sorry. His poor wife! He'd got two children, too, hadn't he, Richard?"

"That's what I'd heard," said Richard Renville, feeling for his pipe. "Bad luck."

"We're just checking that nothing had happened to upset Mr. Fent at the dinner party." Sloan said his party piece glibly. He and Crosby had moved down Constance Parva High Street from Miss Paterson's cottage to King's Tree House where the Renvilles lived. He wouldn't be surprised if the bee hadn't come too.

"Oh, no, it was a lovely evening." Ursula Renville ushered the two policemen into chairs. "The table looked charming and the food was so nice. I don't know why a meal you haven't cooked yourself tastes so much nicer but it does."

"What did you have?" asked Sloan encouragingly.

She told him and it tallied.

"An interesting pudding," observed Sloan.

"Wasn't it?" she agreed happily. "French. A speciality of the Dauphinois district. That's where Bill and Helen went for their holidays. They had crémets there and that's why Helen wanted to try it herself. She was so taken with it that Bill bought her a set of the little dishes. She showed them to me once."

"Special ones with holes," said Crosby.

"Yes." She smiled at him and nodded. "Heart-shaped." Almost absent-mindedly she produced excellent coffee and set it before the policemen without asking. "You make a sort of milk curd, I think . . ."

"And drain it through muslin," supplemented Crosby.

"How clever of you to know," she beamed at the detective constable.

"Did they turn out well?" growled Sloan. Anyone listening to Crosby would think he was a Cordon Bleu cook, while Sloan knew for a fact that he couldn't even boil a kettle, let alone an egg.

"Except one," said Mrs. Renville. "They were standing on the sideboard when we went into the dining-room and I did happen to notice that one had collapsed just the tiniest bit at one edge."

"Who had that, I wonder?" murmured Sloan half-aloud. He couldn't himself think of anything better for pudding than one of his wife's apple pies—she hadn't needed those cookery books for wedding presents—but there was no accounting for taste, and anything—but anything—consumed that night at Strontfield might matter.

Richard Renville tapped his pipe against an ash-tray and said ruefully, "If it's anything like this house, Inspector, I can tell you straightaway who got the failure put in front of him. The host."

"Nonsense, darling," said his wife roundly. "The hostess always has the things that don't turn out right." She smiled at the two policemen. "Men make such a fuss if you give them anything that isn't perfect, don't they? I bet poor Helen ate it."

Renville shook his head. "Not that time. You can take it from me, Inspector, that it was Bill who had that collapsed crémet. I remember because I saw it on his tray and not on Helen's."

"There were two trays, were there, sir?" prompted Sloan.

"That's right." Renville nodded. "With six crémets on

each. Bill served his end of the table and Helen hers. There was a bowl of raspberries at each end and cream if you wanted it. It was all nicely done, you know. No fuss."

It was Sloan's turn to nod agreement. No, there had been no fuss.

And it had all been nicely done.

Someone had somehow seen to it that Bill Fent had had a potentially fatal dose of a soluble barbiturate in the presence of eleven other people, one of whom was presumably the murderer, though they couldn't even be sure about that yet, not with Peter Miller Fent in the offing. Very much in the offing, especially last Saturday night.

"The drink," said Sloan, improving upon the shining hour.

Renville frowned. "Bill hadn't had too much or anything like that."

"I understand, sir, that the gentlemen took some port."

"We did indeed." The man's frown vanished and his face lit up. "You know, Inspector, when I heard about poor Bill I was glad for him that that port was the last thing he had to drink."

"Good, was it, sir?"

"Superb," said Renville reverently. "Bill's father laid a pipe of it down the year Bill was born. A fine old English custom . . ."

"Like wetting the baby's head?" asked Crosby intelligently.

Renville blinked at him. "In a way, I suppose. No good, of course, if the baby comes in a bad year."

"Naturally," agreed Sloan gravely. "May we take it, then, that Mr. Fent was born in a good year?"

"According to the professor it was the last of the good years"—Renville grinned—"but the professor's like that. Getting on, you know, and a bit of a pessimist these days."

It was Sloan's experience that the two often went together. "What year would it have been, sir?"

"'Thirty-five. Actually," Renville said, "'forty-five was a good year too, but the professor wouldn't have it. Said 'thirty-one was better still. The good old days and all that."

"Really, sir?" The only year—the only day—that Kitty, Kitty bothered about down in The Dog and Partridge was the current one.

"Bill said it was coming to the end of its drinkability but"—Richard Renville clenched his pipe between his teeth—"I must say it went down very well."

So it did, Sloan was sure, in The Dog and Partridge in Railway Street.

Every night.

The burly businessman sighed. "Quite an occasion, really."

"What did you talk about?"

He laughed. "Believe it or not we talked about blood donors. Washby was trying to enrol us all—except Marchmont. He was one already. There's some sort of team doing the county next month . . ."

"There now!" exclaimed his wife. "We thought you'd be talking about us."

"Well," challenged Renville, "what did you talk about?"

"Jam."

"Well, then . . ."

Sloan said, "The port—I take it that all the gentlemen had some?"

"I should jolly well think so," said Renville spiritedly. "Good Lord, Inspector, you wouldn't pass up vintage port at Strontfield—you'd be mad."

"Sorry, sir," said Sloan humbly. Kitty, Kitty would never have asked.

He had just one more question for them. Had either of the Renvilles been up to the Park to see Helen Fent since Bill had been killed.

Both shook their heads.

"Wait a minute, though," Ursula put out a hand. "I do

know who was going to go. Marjorie Marchmont. Yesterday evening. She mentioned that she intended to walk up
to Strontfield to see Helen later. I remember that because
she said that she thought people felt just as flat after a funeral as they did after a wedding . . ."

She paused. "I can't have got that the right way round,
can I?"

"Yes, madam." Some of the superintendent's Winter
Evening Class on Sociology had rubbed off on them all at
the Police Station. "They're both Rites of Passage."

"Really?" The vague look had come back to Ursula's
face.

A few minutes later Crosby pulled the police car out of
the King's Tree House drive and turned back into Constance Parva High Street. As he did so a small green car
slowed down, its indicator blinking its intention of turning
off the village High Street and into the Renvilles' driveway.

"Well, what do you know?" drawled the constable
phlegmatically. "Young Mr. Quentin Fent, the country
landowner, coming to call upon Mr. Richard Renville,
property company director."

"And," said Sloan, "they're growing beet-root in their
cabbage patch."

THIRTEEN

Detective Inspector Sloan's approach at the doctor's house was more business-like. There were no bees here and no coffee either. The action—as Crosby would have put it—was all at the side of the house: outside the garage. It was Saturday morning and the doctor, dressed in his oldest clothes, was cleaning his car. He straightened up as he saw the two policemen and tossed the wash-leather into a bucket of water.

Sloan told him about Exley's dying. "We may need you at the resumed inquest on Mr. Fent, Doctor."

Dr. Washby gave a quick jerk of his head. "Right."

"To give evidence as to his condition before he left the house and so forth," went on Sloan easily. "You know the sort of thing."

"I do." The doctor wrung the wash-leather out and applied it to the bonnet of the car. "Sorry I can't stop doing this. I'll have to hose it all down again if it dries off before I can leather it."

"Carry on," said Sloan largely.

"You'll be letting me know about the inquest then, won't you?"

"We will, Doctor. We've always got the professor, of course, as the last person to see the deceased alive, but he's not young and I think your observations would carry more weight."

"Naturally anything I can do . . ." Paul Washby drew the chamois leather carefully down the bonnet toward the radiator. "I wish there was something a bit more useful than just standing up at an inquest and saying that Bill seemed perfectly normal to me."

"Were you sitting near him?" inquired Sloan casually.

"Me? No, I was up at the other end of the table. Between Helen Fent and Miss Paterson. Veronica was, though. Hang on and I'll give her a call."

"Bill?" said Veronica Washby merging from the kitchen door in a very pretty apron, and greeting them. "Yes, I was sitting on his left. He seemed quite all right to me—not that I knew him really well or anything. Such a nice man. It's all so sad, isn't it?"

"Yes, madam," agreed the policeman. Sad, mad, bad . . . perhaps it didn't matter which word you used.

"He teased the professor a lot but ever so nicely and you could see he was enjoying it."

"The professor was near you too?"

"Oh, yes, on my other side. He's sweet, isn't he?"

"And you'd be opposite . . . ?"

"Mrs. Renville."

"Ah, yes." Full marks, thought Sloan silently, to his wife, Margaret. She'd been right about the seating then. "You'd have Mr. Marchmont on your other side perhaps?" he ventured.

"Yes, I did." She hesitated. "He didn't say a lot, though."

There was a guffaw from her husband. "Never worry, Marjorie talked enough for two at our end of the table. You should have heard her laugh when we got on to the development and I told her that hoary old chestnut about a smell in the village. Have you heard it, Inspector?"

"No," said Sloan firmly.

"It went like this. Old lady to countryman: 'Can it be the drains?' Countryman to old lady: 'Can't be the drains, mum, 'cos there ain't any.'"

An immoderate laugh escaped Constable Crosby.

"Glad you like it." Washby grinned. "Our Miss Paterson didn't. She went a bit Queen Victoria over it. Not amused and all that. You know she was dead against the drains, don't you, because of the development?"

"Progress does bring problems," said Sloan with meticulous fairness. "How did you find Mr. Marchmont, Mrs. Washby?"

"I think he's a bit shy," said Veronica Washby, "though he did tell Annabel Pollock—she was opposite him—how nicely she'd done the flowers."

Dr. Washby turned to Sloan and said sardonically, "Flower arrangements are a bit competitive in Constance Parva, Inspector. Now over in Constance Magna they go in for blood sports more."

"And cricket," his wife reminded him.

"And cricket," agreed the doctor. "There's a real needle match today, Inspector. The Constances' annual battle. Constance Parva versus Constance Magna." He drew the wash-leather over the nearside wing of his car and pointed up at the cloudless sky. "If the weather breaks they'll say I've made it rain by cleaning my car. And if I go around in a dirty car they'll say I'm a lousy doctor. Can't win, can you?"

"Not often, sir," said Sloan, taking his leave.

Peter Miller stood on the front doorstep of Strontfield Park, his hat dangling uncertainly between his fingers. Annabel Pollock answered the door.

"Come to apologize," he mumbled, introducing himself. "Say I'm sorry and all that."

"What for?" Annabel collected herself rapidly and said, "I mean—do come in, Mr. Miller, and tell me what you're sorry about."

"My Jersey cows—the whole herd must have got into the Park again. Last night, I think. We had to get them out for the morning milking."

"Oh." A look of relief passed over her face. "Is that all?"

"But it's not the first time it's happened," said the farmer. "Bill said he'd get some spiles from Greg Fitch and do something about the fence, but naturally . . ."

"Naturally," concurred Annabel.

"I should have done something myself, really," he said quickly, "seeing that . . . in the circumstances."

"I don't suppose they've done any harm." The nurse's instinct to reassure was well to the fore.

"That's just it," he said twisting his lips awkwardly. "They have."

"In the Park? I don't see what they could . . ."

He hesitated. "They got round by the Folly."

"They couldn't very well knock that down, Mr. Miller."

"They haven't. Not the Folly." He cleared his throat and began again. "You know the statue at the end of the walk there?"

"I do." Annabel's lips twitched ever so slightly. "We used to call it Naughty Nigel when we were small."

"It's a faun, I think." Miller's face crumpled into a responding grin. "Or Eros, perhaps."

"The god of love?" She nodded. "Could be. Old Fitch didn't approve of it, you know. Whenever he was working that way he would hang his jacket over its shoulders." Annabel giggled. "That made it seem so much worse somehow. What have they done to it?"

"I think one of them knocked it off its pedestal."

"Cloven hooves shouldn't have upset it, I suppose."

"But they did," said Miller solemnly.

"Fitch will be pleased."

"Mrs. Fent might not be."

"Don't worry," said Annabel comfortingly. "Somehow I don't think she'll mind all that much now."

"Of course," mumbled Miller suddenly contrite. "Got other troubles now, hasn't she?"

The nurse nodded.

"Had I better see her and explain?"

"No." Annabel shok her head decisively. "She doesn't want to see anyone. She's still very upset."

"Quite understand," said Miller immediately. "Not surprising, really." He paused. "Will she stay on?"

"I don't think," said the girl, "that she's made any plans yet."

"It's early days, of course," agreed the farmer. "Difficult and all that . . ."

They were interrupted by the crunch of car tyres on the drive outside and the sound of someone stepping up to the front door. Peter Miller began to move. "I'd better go. You've got more visitors. I always seem to call just as someone arrives . . ."

Annabel murmured something politely deprecating as she showed him the door. But she looked thoughtful. "So you do, Mr. Miller," she said to herself as she showed him out, "so you do."

The new arrival was Professor Berry, his transport an archaic taxi from Larking. He patted his chest and wheezed, "We're both a bit long in the tooth but we've made it." He stood in the doorway and called back to the driver, "Won't be long, Wilson. Make yourself comfortable." He turned to Annabel. "I've just come to pay my respects to Helen. How is she?"

"Better than yesterday."

"Good."

"Come and sit down." She shepherded him into a chair.

"And how are you managing?" he inquired when he'd got his breath back.

"All right so far, Professor, but I have to go back to the hospital on Monday. My holiday's over."

"Not much of a holiday for you, Annabel, I'm afraid."

She shrugged her shoulders. "Can't be helped. It's worse for Helen. In a way, you know, I'm glad that I was here for Bill's last week. I've always enjoyed my holidays at Strontfield and when I was small—when we were in India—

it meant England to me. Now"—she sighed—"now I don't suppose I'll be invited any more—anyway it'll all be different."

"But surely . . ."

"Quentin's no relation of mine," she said stiffly. "It's Bill who was my cousin and not on the Fent side at all. I'm no Fent."

"Of course." He subsided. "I was forgetting."

"Not even a remote connection," she said firmly.

"I expect," puffed the old man, "you'll still keep in touch with Helen, though."

"I expect so," she said perfunctorily. "At the moment, I must say, Helen doesn't seem to want to see me or talk to me or to anyone else. She's been shut up in her room since the funeral. With the door locked, too. And she won't even answer the telephone. 'Don't put any calls through on the bedroom extension,' she said yesterday. 'No matter who rings.' What am I to do?"

"Whatever she asks," said the professor placidly. "It's usually the easiest thing." He looked at her over the top of his glasses. "With women particularly." He was a bachelor.

"But what reason could she have . . ."

"Probably none at all," said the old gentleman. "There doesn't have to be, you know." He gave her a benevolent smile. "The human race isn't rational and doesn't do what it does do for what we are pleased to call reasons. Motives, perhaps, but not always those, either."

"Whatever it is," she responded with some asperity, "I don't feel that I can go off tomorrow night back to St. Ninian's leaving Helen locked up in her room."

"What about Quentin?"

"He's got another week's holiday and Helen's asked him not to go." She waved a hand in a gesture which embraced the house and park. "There are things to be attended to and Mr. Puckle, the solicitor, wants to see him on Monday morning in his office."

"So he's staying?"

"Oh, yes, he's staying all right, but he's no cook or nurse. I expect," added Annabel shrewdly, "that he'll want his precious Jacqueline to see Strontfield, though."

"Not without an invitation, I hope," said the professor. "That would be too much."

"Oh, no. Not even Quentin would do that. Besides," went on Annabel fairly, "to do her justice, I don't think Jacqueline would come without one from Helen. Delicacy of feeling may not be the Battersby family's strong suit but she's not as insensitive as all that."

"That's good," said Berry. "Especially as I understand from Quentin that they're getting married on the strength of Strontfield."

"The day has been named anyway," said Annabel Pollock in such studiously neutral tones that the professor looked up at her in surprise.

Detective Inspector Sloan balanced his notebook on his knee as Crosby started up the police car for the homeward journey to Berebury.

"We're getting on, Crosby," he remarked. "We know what they all had to eat now and—"

"Did you say 'eat,' sir? What a good idea. My landlady doesn't know the meaning of breakfast."

"And," continued Sloan, unmoved, "we know whereabouts at the table everyone was sitting."

"What we don't know," said Crosby unhelpfully, "is which course had the poison in."

"I wonder," said Sloan.

"Sir?"

"Think, Crosby, think." Teach him, they said at the station, and he'll learn. Sloan wasn't so sure.

The constable steered the car out of the village toward the open road. "It wasn't the drink for a start. Those bottles . . ."

"Can be forgotten. It wasn't the drink. Unless it was the coffee. The wine and the port came out of bottles shared by everyone."

"We could test the port just to make sure."

"We could not," said Sloan flatly. "Not without a warrant we couldn't. Keep going."

Crosby rightly interpreted this last to refer to his detective speculations rather than his driving. The car was travelling quite fast enough anyway. He said, "It couldn't very well have been the meat and vegetables, sir. Or the cheese, come to that."

"Agreed," said Sloan promptly. "I don't see that it would be possible to poison just one serving of the roast or the trimmings or the cheese."

"That leaves the soup and the pudding, sir." He glanced in his rear-view mirror. "Am I getting warmer?"

"You are." Sloan sighed. He wasn't going to learn. Not this one. Not if he didn't know by now that this wasn't "Hunt the Thimble" but murder.

"The soup and the pudding, then, sir."

"And what is it that makes them more likely, anyway?"

A prodigious frown settled on Crosby's brow. "Don't know, sir."

"They were the only items served in individual dishes," said Sloan patiently, "and laid out in the dining-room before the meal began."

"Oh, I get it." The frown cleared. "Eleven O.K. One laced with whatever it was."

"A soluble barbiturate." Sometimes he didn't know why he bothered.

"Soup or sweet . . ." Crosby negotiated the last of Constance Parva High Street and started to pick up real speed.

"There is a possibility," said Sloan carefully, "that we could get nearer than that."

Crosby changed gear for a hill. "Sir?"

"Cucumber is not noted for its strong flavour."

"Hardly worth eating, if you ask me," said the constable candidly. "Nothing to it. No taste at all."

"Precisely," said Sloan. "So?"

"So," said Crosby after due pause for thought, "seeing as how the analyst said this stuff . . ."

"A soluble barbiturate," said Sloan between clenched teeth.

". . . tasted bad we come to the pudding."

"We come to the pudding," agreed Sloan. Journey's end. A pudding. A thimble hunted for and found.

"It must have tasted pretty grim to begin with, sir, on its own even without any stu . . . soluble barbiturate." He screwed up his face. "Curds of sour cream! Ugh!"

"Let us say," murmured Sloan, "that the flavour was what is called pronounced."

"One spoonful would have been enough for me, sir, I can tell you."

"You are forgetting, Crosby, that these people there that night would probably have enjoyed it and if they didn't enjoy it they would still have eaten it."

"Cor . . ."

"And there was one person there who would have eaten it if it killed him," said Sloan, "whatever it tasted like."

"Who was that, sir?"

"The husband of the woman who made it," said Sloan, worldly-wise and married.

"Really, sir?"

"You're still a bachelor, Crosby, aren't you?"

"Yes, sir. Though if Mrs. Pennyfeather . . ."

"The poisoning," said Sloan briskly. "Now, then, how was it done?"

Crosby practically came to attention at the wheel. "Something put in the crémet?"

"Probably. Which one?"

"The collapsed one," said the constable at once.

"Why that one?"

"Because they couldn't get the poison in without breaking it?"

"No," said Sloan. "The poison, I should say, went over it. It was soluble, remember. No, I should think it was broken for a different reason."

Crosby slowed down and turned into a major road and immediately picked up speed.

"Go on, Crosby. Work it out for yourself."

"Was it," he began uncertainly, "collapsed to make sure that the right person had the doctored one?"

"I think so. Though," said Sloan conscientiously, "that leaves us with one big difficulty."

"Which was the right person?" offered Crosby.

"Exactly. From the way things were I think whoever damaged one of those puddings could only be sure that either the host or hostess had it. Granted one of them would be bound to . . . which is a bit tricky, to say the least."

"Not if it didn't matter which of them had it," said Crosby, taking the literal view.

"True," said Sloan mildly. "I think we'll have to get a little nearer than that for the Prosecution. Now, there's something else we'll have to establish . . ."

"Whether the twelfth crémet collapsed before or after it was put on the sideboard . . ." finished Crosby for him.

"Well done," said Sloan, meting out praise where praise was due. He stared out of the car window. "And as I see it there's only one way to go about that."

Crosby groaned. "Not Milly again, sir? Anything but that."

"Duty calls, Crosby." He grinned. "Besides, you're the younger man. You've got longer to live."

"I'm not sure that I have," protested the constable. "Not with those brothers of hers on the war-path. And then there's her mum."

"Courage," said Sloan bracingly. "Remember there's always the Police Widows and Orphans' Fund behind you."

"But I'm not married," wailed Crosby, "like I said."

All the bells were down when Sloan and Crosby got back to Berebury Police Station. Superintendent Leeyes was sitting in his office drumming his fingers on his desk.

"Something's happened," he snapped.

Sloan waited.

"One of your dinner party people," he said.

"Yes?" said Sloan.

"Gone missing."

FOURTEEN

"Who, sir?"

Superintendent Leeyes squinted down at a message pad. "A party by the name of Marchmont. Mrs. Marjorie Marchmont."

"The fat one," said Sloan. "She's on our list but we didn't get as far as her house this morning."

"Pity," said Leeyes. "She hasn't been seen since yesterday evening."

"Her husband?"

"Her husband didn't come home last night."

Sloan pricked up his ears.

"Or so he says," added Leeyes portentously. "He says he got back home this morning to an empty house with no wife and every sign of no wife having been there last night either."

"Every sign?"

"Empty milk bottles not put out," recited Leeyes, "bed cold, cat not fed . . ."

Sloan's mind drifted away from the superintendent's bare office. How was it that William Shakespeare had put the duties of a wife—"To keep with you at meals, comfort your bed, and talk with you sometimes." Somebody—his father-in-law, perhaps, it would have been like him—had quoted it at Sloan's own wedding and the ladies, he remembered, had been rather shocked.

"And the newspapers and morning post not taken in," continued Leeyes prosaically. "It all adds up to no wife, Sloan . . . Sloan, are you listening to me?"

"Yes, sir. Of course, sir. I was just thinking about the husband. A thin, weedy chap."

"So was Crippen," said Leeyes darkly.

"Where was he last night?"

"Ah," said Leeyes, "he was at a Regimental reunion dinner in Calleford. The East Calleshires. He always goes."

"And he stayed the night?"

"So he says, so he says. It sounds to me," added the superintendent complacently, "as if he had a touch of the Happy Harry's."

"Breath test fever." It was a disease that didn't do any harm. On the contrary . . .

"Didn't want to risk a d.i.c. check, anyway," said Leeyes. "Regimental Reunion dinners aren't exactly Band of Hope affairs, you know, Sloan."

Sloan did know. The whole of Berebury Police Station had to mind its step for a couple of days each year after the superintendent had splashed his way ashore at Walcheren all over again—with gestures.

He opened his notebook. "Where did her husband say he stayed, sir?"

"The Tabard in Bear Street."

"P.c. Bargrave hasn't been to the house himself yet," explained Sloan to Crosby as they returned to Constance Parva with all possible speed. "He remembered that Mrs. Marchmont was one of the twelve at the dinner party and sent for us instead."

"One went to Heaven and then there were eleven," chanted Crosby mordantly.

Sloan grunted. He knew it. Nursery rhymes and nursery games were just about Crosby's level.

"And now there are only ten, sir." The constable slammed the car into top gear and put his foot down.

"It could be a false alarm," Sloan reminded him. But he didn't think so.

He was even less inclined to think so after he had spoken to Daniel Marchmont.

"It's just not like my wife, Inspector," he kept on saying over and over again. "If anything had happened she would have left a note for certain. She was always leaving notes for me. Funny ones, mostly. With drawings." He looked embarrassed. "Actually, I've kept most of them though she doesn't know that."

"So, sir," said Sloan in a business-like fashion, "you think that we can assume that wherever she went she expected to be home before you?"

"Oh, yes," said Marchmont. "Definitely."

"She didn't mind being in the house alone?"

"Good Lord, no." He practically threw his chest out on his wife's behalf. "Marjorie wasn't like that, Inspector. She wasn't frightened of anything. Anything or anybody."

Sloan was sorry to hear it. Decent fear kept a lot of people out of trouble. "When did you last see her, sir?"

"Lunch-time yesterday." He smiled jerkily. "We went to the funeral, of course, and then went back to the Washbys' to eat. They asked Professor Berry back too. He's a bit frail, you know."

"And after that?"

"I went back to my office in Berebury—I'm an accountant, you know. I didn't come home until this morning"—he looked round helplessly—"and she wasn't here."

"I see, sir. And the house was—er—as usual?" A cheerful untidiness had prevailed in all the rooms Sloan had seen so far.

"Oh, yes," the accountant nodded. "This isn't the sort of house where you couldn't put a newspaper down . . ."

"Quite so, sir." From where Sloan stood the disorder was such that it looked as if the problem would be—when you had put it down—finding it again in the general confusion. "And after you left your office, sir?"

"I went straight to Calleford for my Regimental Dinner.

There didn't seem a lot of point in hacking my way out to Constance Parva again and then going on to Calleford the country way when I could do it all in half the time and twice the comfort by motorway."

"Quite so, sir." The Calleshire stretch of the London motorway was Inspector's Harpe's pride and joy. "By the way, sir, in the—er—the ordinary course of events would the late Mr. Fent have been going to this dinner too?"

"Bill? Oh, no, Inspector. Bill was too young for the war and then when National Service came in he was too busy trying to make a go of Strontfield as a farm. I should say he would have been exempt."

"I see, sir. Thank you." Sloan closed his notebook. "And you have no idea where Mrs. Marchmont might be?"

"None," said the little man miserably. "And she's down to do the church flowers at three."

For once Crosby didn't ask for orders as he climbed into the driving seat of the police car. Without comment he drove out of the lane where the Marchmonts lived, and down the length of Constance Parva High Street, past the doctor's house, past King's Tree House where the Renvilles lived, past Miss Paterson's cottage, round by St. Leonard's church, and finally turned the car sedately through the gates of Strontfield Park.

Sloan made no attempt to stop him.

So it was that when at long last Detective Inspector Sloan and Detective Constable Crosby did set foot inside Strontfield Park it was to inquire after a missing woman. And that was not before they had noticed and—police-fashion—duly noted that the little green car in which Quentin Fent had visited the Renvilles was back again and parked in front of the house.

Quentin himself received them and waved them authoritatively into arm-chairs in the drawing-room. A not-so-subtle change had overtaken Quentin Fent between yesterday

and today. Gone was the subordinate mourner; even the
"enfant terrible" was no more. Nor was the sophisticated
West End art expert much in evidence. And as for the im-
pecunious young man holidaying with relations, there was
not a single sign.

"Tell me, gentlemen, what I can do for you," he said.

For a long moment Sloan was afflicted with a deep sense
of *déjà vu*. He didn't answer Quentin but sat quite still,
feeling about in his memory, trying to locate something.
Somewhere and at some time he had seen this change
come over a young man overnight before. And then it
came to him.

Constable Middleton made sergeant. Over Easterbrook
way.

A fairy godmother's wand couldn't have wrought a
greater change in stature between one day and the next. An
inch in height at least for each stripe—to say nothing of
chest measurements bigger by far. And every remark
weightier forever afterwards.

"Do for us, sir? Oh, yes," Sloan collected himself and explained about Marjorie Marchmont. "We understand
from Mrs. Renville that Mrs. Marchmont proposed to
come here yesterday evening to visit Mrs. Fent."

"Well, she didn't get here," said Quentin immediately.
"Or if she did I didn't see her." He grinned. "Not likely to
miss her, are you, if she is around. Not at that size."

"No, sir."

"And if she did come," said Quentin confidently, "she
wouldn't have got near Helen for sure."

"No, sir?"

"She's been mewed up in that bedroom of hers ever
since Bill's funeral." He shrugged his shoulders. "Annabel
can't do anything with her. She won't see anyone. She
won't even talk to anyone on the telephone so you can bet
your bottom dollar that she wouldn't have seen Marjorie
Marchmont, of all people."

"Of all people?" Sloan let the phrase hang.

"Well," he stirred restively, "you couldn't exactly call her peaceful company for a start, could you? There's her laugh for a start. And a bull in a china shop could beat her for tact any day of the week."

"Spoke her mind, did she, sir?"

"Rain or shine, you might say," replied Quentin Fent. "You know what people like that are like."

Sloan nodded. The trouble with people who said what they thought was that they didn't always think a lot. "Did she . . ."

But Quentin had gone back to grumbling about his cousin's widow. "And all that Annabel can get Helen to eat is tinned peaches—oh, and tea. Seems," he went on plaintively, "as if we're taking fresh pots up there every ten minutes."

Sloan, veteran observer of more domestic tragedies than he cared to remember, said, "Tea is a great stand-by, sir." He coughed discreetly and added, "Better than the bottle."

"What? Oh, yes, of course. No worries there. Actually, I don't think Helen's had anything to drink at all since I've been down here, now you come to mention it. No, it's that she won't see anyone."

"No one?"

"No one at all. Not even me," said Quentin somewhat naïvely, the small boy showing for a fleeting moment, "let alone Marjorie Marchmont."

Sloan let the touch of egoism pass. "Just Miss Pollock?" he said.

"She's different. She's a nurse." Quentin Fent dismissed Annabel Pollock as having the universal *laissez-passer* of her profession. "But do you know since the funeral—that's when she got too upset—Helen's only seen me once."

"Indeed?"

"And then all she said was to see Mr. Puckle about everything."

"Well, he is . . ."

"I don't want to be insensitive and all that," went on Quentin, "but hang it all, it's all going to be mine in under three weeks."

"Perhaps," murmured Sloan, "that's what Mrs. Fent is finding so hard to bear."

"Could be, but," said Quentin importantly, "there are things to be done on an estate of this size and some of them need doing now."

"Like the development?"

Quentin flushed. "I can't afford to let the grass grow under my feet, Inspector. In fact," he said neatly, "I can't afford to let the grass grow full stop. That land has got to grow bricks if Strontfield is going to stay solvent. There was nothing wrong with the scheme that Renville drew up, you know. Even Bill said so."

"You're going to go ahead with it then, sir, are you?"

"Too soon to say," said Fent shutting up like a clam. "Now what's all this about Marjorie Marchmont being hard to find?"

Annabel Pollock, when appealed to, proved more helpful. "I certainly didn't see Mrs. Marchmont last night, Inspector, and I'm sure Helen didn't because she stayed in her room all evening . . . no, I'm wrong. She didn't."

This was obviously news to Quentin as well as to Sloan.

"She came downstairs," said Annabel, "just before bedtime—at least that's when I bumped into her."

"Where?" asked Sloan.

"Near the garden door. She was worried about its being locked for the night."

"And was it?"

"She said so. I didn't check. Then she went back to bed."

Sloan said, "When was this?"

"Just before ten, I think. It was while Quentin was on the telephone."

"To my fiancée," said Quentin proprietorially.

"Of course," went on Annabel, "Mrs. Marchmont might have come up to the house earlier and not got an answer." She hesitated. "I did slip out for a few minutes about eight o'clock. Helen wouldn't have heard the bell in her bedroom."

"And she wouldn't have answered it if she had," added Quentin petulantly.

"Mr. Fent here would have heard it, though," pointed out Sloan.

Annabel shook her head. "Not if she'd come while he was out."

"You were out too then were you, sir?" said Sloan at his silkiest.

Quentin looked distinctly sulky. "Only if you can call walking in my ow . . . in the Park being out."

"And did you see anyone while you were—er—out?"

"What's that to . . ."

"The same person," swept on Sloan smoothly, "might have seen Mrs. Marchmont."

"Saw Peter Miller, as a matter of fact," he said huffily. "We—er—happened to meet down by the gates. He's the farmer next door."

"Oh, he was in the Park too, was he?" Out of the corner of his eye Sloan could see Crosby making a note of that.

"Just for a chat, Inspector." Quentin Fent had hit his stride again now. "He seems a sensible sort of chap. He wanted to know my intentions naturally. He's got land that's ripe for development too. He reckons if I put up something down near the village he'll get planning permission for the part of his land that's next door to it. It's no more good for farming than Strontfield is."

"And neither of you saw anyone else in the Park?"

Quentin shook his head but Annabel Pollock said, "I did. Only in the distance, but I think I recognized him by his dog."

"Who?"

"Richard Renville. He was taking Spot for a walk through the Park. It's a Dalmation."

"It is permitted? This exercising of dogs in the Park?"

"Can't stop it," said Quentin promptly.

"There's an old Right of Way," said Annabel.

"Been there since time immemorial and all that," said Quentin. "We can't close it."

Sloan noted the Royal pronoun and asked innocently, "What if the development comes?"

"We can apply to divert it. Actually I think Renville's plan lets it run between some houses."

"I see, sir." One thing was certain. Quentin Fent hadn't wasted any time since his cousin Bill had died. Sloan stood up. "Now if we might just have a word with Mrs. Fent . . ."

"I'm sorry, Inspector." Annabel shook her head regretfully. "She won't hear of it."

He'd never been one for head-on clashes, not even as a young constable. Now he was an inspector he always looked for a way round. It was quicker. "Well, thank you both for seeing me. Now we must get on with finding Mrs. Marchmont."

He expanded on this theme to Crosby on their way down the drive. "We need some help on this. It'd take all day to go over this place and grounds alone and we need to see Mr. Peter Miller Fent . . ."

Crosby gazed out of the car window. "And we don't know that she actually got here, do we, sir?"

"Only that Mrs. Renville said she said she was coming," said Sloan briefly. "That's all we really know. That and the fact that we've got to find her. Quickly."

In the event a small Norfolk terrier called Rags beat them all to it.

It was toward the end of the afternoon and Sloan was back at the Police Station planning a large-scale search.

Saturday afternoon in the nature of things was not the best day for this. True, volunteer labour was available—excepting those who were hitting a ball on a cricket pitch—but the professionals were busy keeping the traffic moving in the Berebury shopping area, policing the county cricket ground in Calleford and letting those who wanted to get to the County Show. This last was in the grounds of Ornum House and a great annual event. Peter Miller, the farmer, was here. At least that was what Sloan had been told at Fallow Farm. So those men who were on duty there were told to keep an eye open for him. Not that that was easy. Saturday was the third and last day and was devoted to the general public who had come *en masse.*

The serious matter of the judging had been accomplished on the Thursday and most of the wrangling over the judges' decisions got over on the Friday. By Saturday roiling passions had died down a little—until the next show —even in the section on pigs.

Landrace Squire Larking the Third, Champion Boar of his class, surveyed the world with pink-rimmed eyes, confident in his glory, never to know how nearly he had come second to Landrace Martin II of Rooden in the next pen. Someone—surely not the owner of Landrace Martin II of Rooden—had scribbled on Landrace Squire Larking the Third's First Prize Certificate:

> Dogs look up to humans
> Cats look down on them
> Pigs is equal.

Rags, the Norfolk terrier, was having a job to look up to his human.

He barked.

Cynthia Paterson called him.

He didn't come.

She called again.

He barked.

Not rabbits, she decided, walking in the direction of the bark. It had come from somewhere near the direction of the Folly. She came out of the trees which surrounded it and saw first of all the fallen statue. Better informed than Annabel Pollock and Peter Miller, and well schooled in a Classical mythology much older than the Christian, she knew it to be Eros himself.

Pausing briefly to consider a Latin tag for the downfall of the God of Love—in a garden, too—she plunged in the direction of the barking.

Rags, she decided, was right inside the Folly.

She called again. When he didn't come she went up to the Folly and looked inside.

And then wished she hadn't.

FIFTEEN

"Brandy," said Annabel Pollock, taking one look at Cynthia Paterson's shocked face. She looked ten years older.

"The police," said Quentin, looking younger and more frightened. "I'll get them straightaway. And the doctor. Here, boy, come over here . . ."

The terrier had obediently followed his mistress over to Strontfield Park. After all, there had been absolutely no response from the large figure on the floor of the Folly. It had remained quite still in spite of all his barking. Rags had soon lost interest and trotted quite happily after Cynthia Paterson as she had stumbled across the Park to the house.

"It's Marjorie," said Cynthia between dry bloodless lips. "I'm sure it's Marjorie. It's her hair."

"Of course," said Annabel soothingly. "You'd know it anywhere."

"It's not that," Cynthia shuddered. "It's what they've done with her hair. Like Porphyria."

"Come and sit down," said Annabel. "Quentin's gone to ring the police."

"Just like Porphyria," repeated Miss Paterson more firmly.

"Quite so," murmured Annabel meaninglessly.

"Poor Marjorie's beautiful hair all round her neck."

"Drink some of this," commanded Annabel.

Obediently the older woman sipped the brandy. "Browning," she remarked in a detached way a moment or so later.

"Browning?"

"Robert, of course," said Cynthia. "Not Elizabeth."

"Have some more brandy," said the nurse practically.

"Don't you know 'Porphyria's Lover'?" asked Miss Paterson. "One of his best poems."

The girl shook her head.

"He strangled her," said Cynthia Paterson shakily, "with her own hair."

As it happened, the village doctor got there fractionally ahead of the police. He'd bumped his car that bit farther over the long grass of the Park than Crosby cared to.

"Dead," said Washby thickly as Sloan reached him. "No doubt about it. Some time ago, too, I should say, though I'm no expert." He turned and raised his voice. "I shouldn't come any nearer, Quentin, if I were you. She's not a pretty sight."

Quentin Fent nodded gratefully and stayed by the car. He seemed diminished by this turn of events.

"Strangled," said the doctor, "with her own hair. Do you want me to . . ."

"No, thank you," said Sloan. "If you would just—er—confirm death we'll do the rest."

"I can do that all right," said Washby unemotionally. "And identify the body, too, if that's any help. Mrs. Marjorie Marchmont."

"That's what I was told," agreed Sloan. "Miss Paterson recognized her too."

Washby dusted his hands and started walking back to his car. Quentin Fent was still standing by it, one hand holding on to the door handle as if the car was a raft on a stormy sea.

"Her husband," said the doctor. "Do you want me to tell him . . ."

"No, thank you," said Sloan again. Most male murderers might be widowers: that didn't mean that the husbands of most murdered women were always murderers, but it did mean that they had to be checked out. First. Fast. "We'll do that."

Washby essayed a wry smile. "Sorry. Of course. Well, in that case I'll go back to the house and take a look at Miss Paterson. Her old heart's not quite so good as she thinks it is." He waved a hand in the direction of the Folly. "Finding Mrs. Machmont won't have done her a lot of good."

"She wants to see you, too, Inspector," put in Quentin. "She said so. Do you want me here now?"

"Not at the moment, sir, thank you," said Sloan. "We'll be along to talk to you all later."

"Well, well, well," drawled Dr. Dabbe as he in his turn stood before the Folly some ten minutes later.

"That's three holes in the ground," murmured Detective Constable Crosby to no one in particular.

The pathologist didn't hear him. He was looking at the statue that was lying on the ground in front of the little building. "Love gone wrong?" he observed quizzically.

"Cows," replied Sloan mundanely. "Or so I'm told. They got into the Park last night from the farm next door." That was something else that would have to be checked as soon as may be. Those cows in the Park last night made an excellent reason for Peter Miller to be in the Park too, last night. If any traces of the young farmer were found round the Folly there was a ready-made reason for them.

Dr. Dabbe seemed unwilling to pass the sculptured figure lying in the grass. "The devil was a fallen angel, Sloan."

"So I understand, Doctor." Sloan himself was in no hurry to go inside the Folly again. Since Dr. Washby left he'd been no nearer, so far, than the entrance and seen to it that no one else had either. Crosby was not going over the floor for footprints. "It's too dry for anything but dust," added Sloan, "though you never know." You never did know either. Not in a case like this. Literally anything might come up.

The pathologist gestured toward the huddled figure lying on the Folly floor. "Do we know—er—who?"

"I'm afraid we do," said Sloan heavily. "Mrs. Marjorie Marchmont. One of the twelve at the dinner party."

"Ah."

"And," plodded on Sloan, "in view of what's happened I think we can assume she would probably have been a material witness for the prosecution . . . if there is a prosecution, that is." He felt suddenly old and tired. "We shouldn't have let this happen."

Pathologists being in the nature of things uninterested in the might-have-been, Dr. Dabbe only craned his neck forward and peered at the body. "Not love gone wrong?"

Sloan shook his head at the euphemism. They had other ones down at the Police Station but they all came to the same thing in the end. "I should be very surprised."

Like a ripple in a pond Crosby was working his way away from the centre of the floor toward the edges. He was somehow contriving to do this without once actively looking at the centrepiece to all the drama. Sloan had observed the same behaviour in his own cat when confronted by a bird too big for it to tackle.

Little birds, yes.

Then it was tail down, body still, and pounce.

But not with a big bird like a sea-gull. It might be only a foot or so away but the cat still wouldn't see it. Nor would it go through the motions of the chase. And I'm as bad, he thought to himself irritably. Thinking about cats instead of about a murderer.

The pathologist altered his stance the better to see. "I don't think, Sloan, that I've ever seen it done this way before."

"Nor me," said Sloan flatly. "And don't want to again,"

he added, battening down the hatches of feeling while still trying to notice the things a policeman should notice.

"Interesting, though," said the pathologist in the tone of a true enthusiast adding a rare species to his collection.

Sloan didn't find it interesting. The dead woman represented to him failure by any yardstick you cared to choose.

"All done, sir," sang out Crosby. He'd finished his crab-like progression over the floor and now he had his back to the inside wall of the Folly. He still wasn't looking at the body on the floor. Sloan didn't blame him. It wasn't a pretty sight. Strangulation never was.

"Thank you," said Sloan. At least Crosby wasn't a converted ghoul. That was something to be thankful for. Inspector Hawkins over at Kinnisport had one of those on his hands. The fellow had fished so many bodies out of the harbour down there that he'd actually got to like it—become a bit of a specialist, so to speak. A defence mechanism, Sloan supposed, but his colleagues still didn't like him for it.

"Why," grumbled Dr. Dabbe, "does this sort of thing always have to happen on a Saturday afternoon?"

"I couldn't say, sir, I'm sure," responded Sloan. And he couldn't, either.

"I couldn't pick on Burns anywhere." Burns was Dr. Dabbe's lugubrious assistant.

Dyson, the police photographer, and his assistant, Williams, had been drummed up, though, and at a signal from Sloan advanced to take their pictures. Behind them an ambulance bumped its way across the Park. The pathologist continued to squint at the body.

"Dead some time, Sloan, I should say."

"Last seen alive toward the end of yesterday afternoon, Doctor." That was something else that would have to be gone into, and soon.

"Could be last night." Dabbe waved a hand at the sadly livid face. "And not poisoning this time."

"Not poisoning," agreed Sloan soberly.

"I wonder why not poisoning," mused the pathologist.

"I think I know why not poisoning," said Sloan. He wasn't sure what he really knew but he was fairly sure about this. "There wasn't time for poisoning to work."

"Ah," Dr. Dabbe lifted his eyebrows. "Time was of the essence, was it?"

"She was going up to the house last night," said Sloan, "to see Mrs. Fent. Or so I'm told."

"And someone didn't want her to?"

"I think that's about the measure of it," agreed Sloan. "Mind you, Mrs. Fent might not have seen her. She's playing hard to get."

"But," Dabbe pointed a finger at the body, "whoever embarked on this might not have known that."

"Might not have been able to count on it," amended Sloan. "The deceased was of—er—a forceful personality. Not over-sensitive, either, from all accounts."

"Ah, I see. Fools rush in where angels fear to tread."

A flash bulb suddenly cast a bright light into the shadows of the Folly. "Now one that way," called Dyson to Williams. "Then I'll take one from floor level." He crouched down and focused his camera on Marjorie Marchmont's head and neck. "I don't think I've ever seen anyone strangled with their own hair before."

"Neither have I," said Sloan, gritting his teeth. If anyone else said that to him he'd . . .

"I took a few of the outside of this place while we were waiting," said Dyson amiably. "Want anything else doing while I'm here?" He gestured toward the fallen statue. "I could do you a nice one of Crosby with his foot on old Nick here. Call it 'Down with All Traitors' and I'd get tenpence a go for it back at the station."

"Not today, thank you," said Sloan. The pathologist, a clear field at last, had already advanced toward the body. He stood for a long moment, silent, considering: a specialist in death and all the thousand ills the flesh is heir to.

"She went quietly," he said at last.

Sloan was surprised and showed it. It didn't sound like Marjorie Marchmont.

"Never knew what hit her," grunted Dabbe. "Taken unawares from behind, I should say. The plaits just crossed over in front and pulled tight. That's all there was to it. Most vulnerable place in the body, of course. It doesn't take much pressure there." The doctor stooped and looked at the dead woman's hands. "No signs of a struggle. Not so much as a broken finger-nail. Someone she knew, at a guess." He straightened up again. "All right, Sloan, you can take her away. I'm finished here now."

Dr. Dabbe might have finished for the time being. Detective Inspector Sloan had only just started.

He dialled the Berebury Golf Club for the fourth time from Strontfield Park. This time he was lucky. Or unlucky. Superintendent Leeyes had now finished his round and was back in the Club-house. The steward would call him to the telephone.

"Can't a man have a round of golf in peace . . ."

Sloan told him about Marjorie Marchmont while he was still grumbling about being disturbed.

"What!" he spluttered.

Sloan said it all over again.

"Dead?" he howled. "The fat woman? You're sure, Sloan?"

Sloan said he was sure. She was dead. She was the fat woman.

"And she was one of your dinner party, wasn't she?"

"She was," said Sloan. First Bill Fent, now Mrs. Marchmont.

"One, two, that'll do," said Leeyes ominously.

"Yes, sir," said Sloan without comment. He was as bad as Crosby, really, with his nursery rhymes.

"Somebody means business, all right," said Leeyes. "All this and poison too."

"We're checking on what everyone was doing last night."

"What they said they were doing," put in Leeyes tartly. "One of them's hardly likely to tell you he was doing for Mrs. Marchmont."

"The husband," went on Sloan sturdily, "seems to be in the clear."

Leeyes grunted at that.

"'The Tabard' in Bear Street, Calleford, say that Daniel Marchmont was there from six-thirty yesterday evening when he registered until after breakfast this morning."

"How do they know he was there all night?" countered Leeyes.

Sloan coughed. "It seems to have been—er—a very short night as far as the hotel was concerned."

Leeyes grunted. "That won't do for the Court. If we ever get to Court with this and I must say . . ."

"The East Calleshires fought at Mallamby Ridge, sir."

"What about it?"

"'Twas a famous victory."

"I know that," snapped Leeyes irritably. "In '44, wasn't it? They stormed the ridge in the face of the enemy."

It had been flat at Walcheren.

"I don't know when they did it for the first time, sir. Apparently they—er—re-enacted it last night."

"In the hotel?"

"At a late stage in the celebrations," said Sloan, quoting a hollow-eyed hotel manager, "their old company commander had an argument with the brigade major about where an abutment had come on the ridge. He decided to prove his point by scaling the staircase well."

"He should have stuck to drawing on the table-cloth."

"Not only the brigade major but the entire company," said Sloan steadily, "decided to pretend that the three flights of stairs were Mallamby Ridge."

"Good God."

"That wasn't all, sir. When they were all off the ground some lunatic remembered that the battle had been fought in the dark and switched all the lights out."

"Where was the manager?" demanded Leeyes militantly.

Sloan cleared his throat. "Unfortunately, sir, I understand that the—er—ploy required an enemy."

"Not . . ."

"All the hotel staff."

"The waiter, the porter, and the upstairs maid, eh, Sloan?"

"The porter went for reinforcements, the waiter hid up in the pantry . . ."

"And the upstairs maid?"

"I'm told the company commander tried to take her hostage but she wasn't having any nonsense like that. She knocked him back a flight."

"And?"

"He still got to the top first. He got the D.S.O. for it at Mallamby," said Sloan, "but he was younger then."

"And our hero?"

"Marchmont? Apparently he took a while to get started, but then he got going too. He made the top all right. Of course he hasn't put the weight on that some of them have. The brigade major, now, he didn't get off the ground at all. Been a pen pusher for thirty years, of course."

"And when this little war game was over?"

"The night porter and the manager put them all to bed."

"That doesn't mean that . . ."

"They are prepared to state that it would have been physically impossible for Marchmont to have driven himself anywhere."

"Are they indeed?" said Leeyes. "Haven't they heard of men pretending to be drunk?"

"Those who actually got to the top," said Sloan, nicely

paraphrasing the manager's choicer epithets for them, "celebrated with champagne. That was when the staff took all their shoes away. All of them. Spares and all."

"But . . ."

"And made sure that no cars got out of the hotel yard. It's an old coaching inn actually, so it was easy to lock up, and to make quite sure the manager drove his own car across the entrance."

"He's had this little problem before then."

"He has." In fact, the whole hotel still sounded in the grips of an almighty hang-over and the manager a bitter man.

"That still leaves everyone except Marchmont, doesn't it, Sloan?"

Sloan agreed.

"It adds up to a lot," said Leeyes profoundly, "but I must say it doesn't amount to much."

Sloan had waited by the Folly until the body of Mrs. Marjorie Marchmont had been borne away in an ambulance to Dr. Dabbe's mortuary. If there was one thing more sinister than an ambulance with a flashing blue light and accompanying warble it was a silent ambulance without a flashing blue light that was travelling scarcely faster than a hearse.

He had watched the vehicle bump its way back to the road and then given himself a mental shake. There was a lot to be done.

He put the telephone down now and turned to his detective constable. "Now, I think, Crosby, we will ask Mrs. Helen Fent to see us."

This time Annabel Pollock agreed without demur. "I'll show you up. This way, Inspector. I've told her about Mrs. Marchmont. I'm sure she'll see you." The girl stopped outside a door on the upstairs landing. She knocked. "Helen, I've brought the inspector up . . ."

There was no response from inside the room.

Annabel knocked again.

"I'm afraid she'll have to see us, miss, whether she likes it or not," said Sloan.

Annabel Pollock put her hand on the door knob with an uneasy laugh. "That's something. It's only shut. She has been keeping it locked . . . Helen, may we come in?"

"Let me go first," said Sloan quickly.

The colour drained out of her face as she stood back and let Sloan enter the room ahead of her.

There was no one there.

SIXTEEN

Sloan had come back to his own office. He doubted if he could have explained why. The proper place for him was undoubtedly the murder headquarters that he'd set up at Strontfield Park.

In the dining-room.

There was a nice irony about that.

In the dining-room at Strontfield Park where the first murder had been perpetrated. That was a good word. As good as "ingested": as good as "noxious substance." Words that meant so much and no more.

He'd wanted a good look at that dining-room anyway, though he was sorry that Marjorie Marchmont had had to die before he had got it. It was Quentin Fent who'd suggested that they use that room as their H.Q. Sloan didn't know whether that meant anything or not, but they'd wanted somewhere and that was where the young man had suggested.

Anyway, Sloan had gone there quickly enough and told Police Constable Bargrave to fit it up as a murder room. But what he'd looked at himself first was the table and chairs. It was an oval table—long and rather narrow—with only room for one chair at the head and one at the foot.

"Aye, there's the rub," he murmured when he looked at the chairs. There was nothing to indicate from the chairs which was the head and which the foot of the table.

P.c. Bargrave, who was old and quiet, looked up but said nothing. If senior police officers chose to talk to themselves that was their affair. He hadn't got where he had—one of

the softest beats in the county—by drawing attention to the
eccentricities of those further up the ladder.

Sloan stood at one end of the long table and rested his
hand on the back of the chair. "Mine host or mine hostess,
I wonder?"

This time Constable Bargrave kept his head down.

Sloan moved over to the sideboard and tried to visualize
two trays of six crémets each standing there. Surely there
must have been something to indicate whether Bill Fent or
Helen Fent—host or hostess—would pick up a certain tray
and thus—in the ordered and polite society by which these
sort of people set such store—have helped themselves to
the fatal dish.

The carving knives.

That would be it.

But not all men carved these days. Could the murderer
have been sure enough to count on it? Or didn't it really
matter which of them died? And had the poison really
been in one of the crémet dishes? It all seemed so very
refined, somehow.

Bargrave had continued to move methodically about the
room seeing to the routine that was as inevitable an outcome of murder as of more humdrum transgressions of the
law. A quiet dog usually made for a quiet flock—that was
true of policemen and people too—but this time there had
been a black sheep a bit too big for such a quiet dog to
handle.

Sloan had left him to it and come back to Berebury.

Over the radio in his office he could hear the message he
wanted going out to all police cars and stations in
Calleshire.

"Attention, all vehicles," said the radio operator unemotionally. The radio gave her voice a nasal twang that it
didn't have in the canteen. "Attention, all vehicles. To
look out for a green Austin Mini car, Registration Number
Yankee Juliet Golf Two One. Believed being driven away

from Strontfield Park, Constance Parva, within the last half an hour. Direction unknown."

"You can say that again," said Crosby. "Did you see Quentin's face when he saw that the car was gone?"

"It is Mrs. Fent's car," said Sloan. Bill Fent's own car hadn't been fit to drive anywhere any more.

"She didn't waste any time, either. As soon as she heard about Mrs. Marchmont she was off."

"She's running away," said Sloan. "She's very frightened. She was frightened before—ever since we went to the funeral. She's even more frightened now that Mrs. Marchmont's dead."

"Frightened of us?"

Sloan looked down not unkindly at his constable. "Probably not."

"Then who . . ."

"If we knew that, then we'd know who did for her husband and for Marjorie Marchmont, wouldn't we?"

The radio interrupted them: "Message continues. The driver is believed to be Mrs. Helen Fent, height five foot five, small build, dark hair. If seen, please stop and question . . ."

"Change that," snapped Sloan suddenly. "Change it to: 'If seen, follow and keep under observation.'"

Crosby leaned over and flipped a switch on the desk. He relayed the message to the Headquarters radio room.

"Attention all vehicles," the curiously nasal voice came out over the air a minute later. "There is a correction to the last 'calling all cars' message . . ."

"If it isn't us she's frightened of," persisted Crosby, "why doesn't she come to us?"

"Good question." Perhaps he was learning after all. "Probably because she doesn't want to tell us the whole story. That's why some people in trouble give us a wide berth . . ."

There was something else Sloan had to do now and he wasn't looking forward to it.

He pointed to the telephone and sighed. "Get me the Golf Club, Crosby."

This time the superintendent took the view that he could blame someone.

Not just someone.

Sloan actually.

"You let her escape?" he howled.

Several pithy rejoinders sprang to Sloan's mind. He rejected them all one by one. Patience might be a virtue. Prudence certainly was.

"We're looking for her now," was all he said.

"Where?"

"Everywhere she could have got to in the time, sir. She can't have been gone long."

"Long enough for her to get out of Calleshire?" the superintendent wanted to know.

Sloan looked at his watch and stopped to think. "If she slipped down to the motorway and put her foot on it I suppose she could be pretty well out of the county by now."

"I hope not," said Leeyes ominously, "that's all. I very much hope not. The assistant chief constable's been onto me about that."

"About what, sir?"

"Overstepping the mark," said Leeyes grandly. "Going over the bounds, if you like."

"Sir?"

"Straying out of your own patch, then," growled Leeyes, "and into the next chap's."

"I'm sure, sir," said Sloan stiffly. "that we should get all possible co-operation from adjacent Forces."

"Well, I'm not," said the superintendent. "Not if last time's anything to go by. The Enderby affair. Remember?"

"Oh, yes, of course . . . but that was different." Sloan understood now. In the Enderby affair Superintendent Leeyes had caused a raiding party over the county boundary in the manner of a marauding Lowland chieftain engaged in a border foray. Calls of "A Percy" were practically audible.

Since patently This Would Not Do, the assistant chief constable had been detailed to reprimand the superintendent. That graceful gentleman had—à la Lady Bracknell —risen from the ranks of the aristocracy, and had taken his idiom from the hunting field.

"Well, I hope you understand now, Sloan," carried on Superintendent Leeyes, "exactly how far you can go after this woman if she leaves Calleshire."

"Yes, I think so, sir."

"When the fox goes into the next hunt's land," said Leeyes heavily, "you can follow it."

"Yes, sir."

"But you mayn't stop earths there."

"No, sir."

"And you mayn't dig."

"No, sir."

"You can kill, though," he added in chilly tones. "That clear?"

"Perfectly, sir."

"Then you're a better man than I am, Gunga Din," said Leeyes frankly. "I thought he was off his rocker."

"Mrs. Fent," said Sloan desperately.

"If she didn't kill her husband . . ."

"We don't know that, sir, yet." The paucity of what they did know was beginning to hit Sloan. "She's in the running, though." She, at least, would have known exactly where Bill Fent was sitting and which crémet would have been his.

"And if she didn't kill this fat woman," swept on Leeyes.

"Dr. Dabbe thinks it was a man who did that."

He was undiverted. "Then she's not running away from us."

"No, sir."

"That means she's running away from somebody."

"Yes, sir."

"And that means," said Leeyes, "she knows something we don't."

"Yes, sir."

"Like who killed her husband if she didn't."

"Like that her husband had been killed by someone else," said Sloan, a chink of light beginning to dawn. "You see, sir, she was perfectly all right until she was told we were at the funeral . . ."

"Told you it was a good idea to go," said Leeyes complacently.

"It's only since then that she went funny and shut herself away."

"That means," said Leeyes, "that she knows who. You'd better find her, Sloan. And quickly."

For a moment Sloan couldn't even remember who Mr. Phillipps was.

"He said you're expecting a call from him, sir," said the policeman on the switchboard.

"Put him through," said Sloan.

He placed the man as soon as he heard his thin reedy voice. It was his friend of the law and the pin-stripe trousers, the clerk to the Lampard Bench.

"You asked this morning, Inspector, if Mr. Fent had ever sentenced anyone who might have borne a grudge against him . . ."

"So I did." Sloan blinked. It couldn't only have been this morning.

"We've been through our records . . ."

"Yes?"

"Not a thing."

"Nobody swearing that they'd get him if it was the last thing they did?" Sloan didn't believe this himself now. Not since he'd seen Marjorie Marchmont lying dead on the Folly floor; but he had to ask.

"No."

"Everybody happy?"

"They mostly thank us," said the clerk defensively.

"So they should," said Sloan briskly. Like most policemen he believed in retributive justice. Punishment should follow crime. People expected it. And punishment did follow crime in all the ordered societies he'd ever heard about. Those that were still going strong, anyway. Presumably those where it didn't had been sunk without trace. "Besides," he added to Mr. Phillipps, "it's what they want."

"I daresay it is," said that worthy. "It's making it fit the crime that's the problem."

"Ah," said Sloan, "the third arm of the law. We're only the second."

"The second?"

"Parliament in its wisdom," said Sloan, "makes the laws. Agreed?"

"Agreed. And very silly some of them are . . ."

"We—the police—for our sins—catch those who don't keep 'em."

"Sometimes," said Mr. Phillipps jovially. "Mostly I should say it's catch-as-catch-can."

"Your lot," continued Sloan, ignoring this, "decide if we did right and they did wrong, and by how much."

"Well . . ."

"And the prison officers—Heaven help them—keep them out of sight and out of mind for as long as you tell them to."

"I suppose," conceded Mr. Phillipps, "we each tend to forget the other three."

"Not always." There was at least one officer in the Berebury Force who kept pinned up on his wall a motto which read: "Far from Court, Far from Care." Found it in a history book, he said, but it did for today, too. "Well, thank you very much, Mr. Phillipps. That's one loop-hole stopped up . . ."

Mr. Phillipps didn't seem quite so keen to ring off.

"You know you mentioned jelly babies this morning," he said uneasily.

"Jelly babies—oh, yes?"

"I always started with their feet. Does it mean anything?"

"I expect so," said Sloan cheerfully, "but I don't know what."

He put the telephone down. That had been, he recognized, a diversion. Welcome, but a diversion for all that.

Besides, it was being borne in upon his mind that there had been an incongruity in something someone—two people, it must have been—had said. A little thing—but significant.

One had said one thing. The other had said something quite different.

Crosby had said something too . . .

The detective constable put his head round the door of Sloan's room and said something now. "They've picked up Mr. Peter Miller stroke Fent at Ornum at the County Show. They're bringing him over to Berebury as quickly as they can."

"Good," said Sloan absently. The man was a piece in the jig-saw puzzle, he was sure about that, but there was more to the picture than just him—unless he had meant to kill Quentin Fent too, and then come in to his inheritance. The difficulty with this sort of jig-saw was knowing what was a piece and what wasn't. Not all of them had neatly interlocking edges; not all had a straight side somewhere to give the picture the defined framework within which the patient solver—you did solve a jig-saw, didn't you? like you solved a crossword—could work away. There was another thing about a real jig-saw. All the pieces fitted somewhere . . .

"I'm going down to the canteen," announced Crosby firmly. "My stomach's beginning to think my throat's cut. Tea and a bun?"

"Please."

He didn't even know if he had all the pieces, let alone what constituted a piece of this particular picture and what was irrelevant. Mrs. Fent's faint—that was part of the whole and so was her shutting herself away and her running away now. But what about her not drinking the wine and her predilection for tinned peaches?

And the development. That always seemed to be cropping up . . .

Sloan paused. That always seemed to be cropping up. Now he came to think of it, there had been one person who always brought it into the conversation. He reached for his notebook to check. That could be a piece of his jigsaw—but it mightn't be.

There were other things, too, which might fit into the Grand Design. It was Napoleon who had had a Grand Design, wasn't it? Well, Bill Fent's murderer had had one too but Sloan was prepared to bet it hadn't included the murder of Mrs. Marjorie Marchmont. And it hadn't included that trip of Fent's late at night over to Cleete with old Professor Berry. No, Bill Fent had been meant to go off to bed to die in his sleep.

Idly Sloan followed through this train of thought. Then what would have happened? He'd have been found dead in bed in the morning, and there would still have been a post mortem unless . . . unless . . .

The door opened. Crosby brought in two mugs of tea.

There had been something, too, that the gardener woman, Miss Paterson, had said about the dinner party . . . the dinner party for the new Mrs. Washby. Something about a fertility rite. And then there was something Richard Renville had told him, too. That they had talked about blood donors after dinner, while the port was going round. A picture was beginning to take shape in Sloan's mind. A different picture from the one they had all been looking at.

That was it. They'd been trying to do the wrong puzzle with the right pieces. Oh, they'd got the pieces all right— all of them—they'd had them all the time, but put together differently they made a very different picture.

"Tea, sir," said Crosby, plonking down the mug.

Sloan didn't even see it. In his mind's eye he was looking again at the broken statue of the God of Love, and hearing Dr. Dabbe's ironic detached voice saying, "The devil was a fallen angel, Sloan . . ."

Then it came to him.

There was just one set of circumstances in which it was immaterial to the murderer whether it was Bill or Helen Fent who died.

And then it was that he guessed why it was that Mrs. Marjorie Marchmont had had to die too.

He reached for the telephone and dialled Mrs. Ursula Renville's number. There was a question that he needed to put to her.

"Who carved last Saturday, Inspector? Why, Bill Fent, of course. He always did. Prided himself on his carving, actually. Anyway, Helen was no good at it. We all knew that."

A murderer was making his way through the quiet streets of Constance Parva. He was going in the direction of the church but that was not where he was really making for. From over beyond the church where the village green was he could hear the inimitable sound—so dear to the cricket commentators—of leather on willow and every now and then the spatter of applause as one of the giants of the village team hit a boundary.

He heard it but it didn't interest him. Rugby had been his game. Not cricket. Definitely not cricket.

He could hear all this because he was on foot. A car was no use to him now; besides, people recognized cars. There was no one much about just now to recognize him. It was

merging from late afternoon to early evening and apart
from the cricketers the village seemed to be at home at tea.
Not that it mattered really if anyone did see him. He
wasn't carrying anything that might make the casual observer think he meant business. Actually, he'd got all he
needed in his jacket pocket, but nobody was to know that.
And he'd got a legitimate reason for his errand if, say, his
victim was not alone.

She was alone, though.

He had reached his destination quite quickly—Miss
Cynthia Paterson's little cottage with its long cat-slide roof
sloping down at the back over the kitchen. He pushed open
the gate. Somewhere Rags, her dog, barked. He closed the
gate carefully behind him and walked round the path.

Miss Paterson was sitting outside on a garden seat, a pot
of tea in front of her. She looked up as his shadow fell
across her face.

"Hullo, Doctor," she said.

Sloan came round the garden path just before the needle
of the disposable syringe met Miss Paterson's flesh. He did
not allow the sight to check his stride but carried on at his
full pace, flinging himself with all the momentum at his
command at Dr. Washby. It wasn't a text-book tackle by
any means but it did the trick.

The needle never went into Miss Paterson. Instead, the
whole syringe fell on to the grass as the doctor reeled before Sloan's weight. It knocked Washby off balance to begin with, but he recovered quickly enough and skipped behind Miss Paterson's chair Crosby, rapidly bringing up the
rear, dodged to one side while Sloan altered course for another charge from the other.

That, at least, was how it seemed.

Two other factors then conspired to alter the situation.
One was a small Norfolk terrier, which, sensing that this
was no formal tea-party but more of a wide game, joined in

the *mêlée* with exacerbating barks and playful nibbles at any male ankle that might be to hand, so to speak. The other was an inexplicable piece of clumsiness on Sloan's part, enacted just as Crosby was about to get a grip of the doctor. It unsighted the constable and diverted his attention for just long enough for Dr. Washby to slip past and make for the gate.

No match in speed for the lighter man, the perspiring constable pounded after him.

Sloan made no move to follow in spite of the fact that sometimes he doubted Crosby's ability to catch anything except a cold.

SEVENTEEN

Sloan sat down on the garden seat beside Miss Paterson.

"Thank you," she said. "You were just in time."

"We should have got here sooner," he said. "He even told me that he was coming to see you. Because of your bad heart."

"But," indignantly, "he's never listened to it."

"I know. That was when the penny dropped."

"He's probably been looking for me all afternoon." She shivered a little and waved a hand toward the Norman tower of St. Leonard's. "I went into the church on my way home. I wanted to think a little after finding Marjorie."

"I think," he said soberly, "that that may have saved your life."

"God moves in a mysterious way . . ."

"Dr. Washby must have realized that you knew something."

"I guessed Bill's part of it anyway." She inclined her head. "Let us say after that I wondered about the rest and then I put two and two together."

"Quicker than I did," said Sloan.

"I knew something that you didn't."

"Oh?"

"I'm old-fashioned," she said. "I still use a lectionary. Always have done."

Sloan waited. He didn't mind people talking about things he didn't understand as long as he didn't have to explain them to Superintendent Leeyes.

"That is to say," she went on, "I always read the Lessons

appointed for the day over to myself before the Morning Service. There's a list of them published every year, you know."

"Yes?" he said encouragingly. Perhaps he wouldn't put any of this in his report. That would be easier than trying to make the superintendent understand it.

"Bill used to read the Lesson in church quite a lot on Sunday mornings," said Miss Paterson. "The first one, usually."

"The squire's job," put in Sloan wryly.

"About the only one left," she agreed. "Well, one Sunday—it must have been a year or so ago—it was the Fifteenth after Trinity—I do remember that . . ."

None of this would do for the superintendent, Sloan decided. Life was too short. "Yes, miss?"

"He should have read Proverbs 17, verse 6."

"And he didn't?" Clues were funny things. You couldn't really begin to define them.

"He read something quite different. I was curious, so when I got home I turned up what he should have read."

"I think I can guess what it was about."

"I don't think he could bring himself to read it aloud—especially with Helen sitting just in front of him."

"No."

"If I remember rightly," said the rector's daughter, "it was a passage about one's children's children being the crown of old men—Revised Version, of course . . ."

"Of course," murmured Sloan.

". . . and a good man leaving an inheritance for his children's children." She paused delicately. "When I realized that he couldn't bring himself to read any of that, I thought I understood why there were no children up at the Park."

"You were right," said Sloan. She had to be right. It was the only explanation which fitted.

She coughed. "Shakespeare had a word for it."

"He would."

"In *Anthony and Cleopatra*."

Sloan wasn't surprised.

"Being unseminar'd, he called it," said Cynthia Paterson.

"All right, Sloan, all right," brayed Leeyes. "I get the message. No need to rub it in." The superintendent never played the nineteenth hole well, but at least he took his time about it and he was still there when Sloan telephoned. "You've lost Washby, and Bill Fent had had mumps at the wrong moment when young and so he couldn't have any children."

"That's what we think," advanced Sloan cautiously. There was a great deal of checking still to be done.

"That doesn't mean that someone had to kill him." Leeyes grunted. "Could happen to anyone," he added as an afterthought.

"It wouldn't have mattered at all," said Sloan, "if his wife hadn't started to have a baby."

"What!"

"That's what we think," repeated Sloan. "Only think, mind you." A chat with Dr. Harriet Baird had produced the bland response that with either her patient's consent or on the judge's specific direction in a court of law and with his protection against proceedings arising out of doing so she would be willing to discuss her patient's condition. Not without. Good afternoon. So he had rung Dr. Dabbe instead and asked him a different question. And got an answer.

Leeyes grunted.

"Everything adds up," said Sloan, "to pregnancy."

"I always understood," boomed Leeyes, "that in cases like Bill Fent's there were—um—ways and means by which the wife could have a baby legally even if it wasn't her husband's."

"Science has made great strides," agreed Sloan hastily. Goodness knows how many people were within earshot at the Golf Club. "But I don't think in this case . . ."

"All traditional, eh, Sloan?"

"Very," said Sloan shortly. Dr. Dabbe had been nearer the mark in asking if it was Love gone wrong. It was.

"And someone knew Bill Fent would be likely to take exception."

"They did. Moreover, that someone stood to lose more than most if this all came out, being a doctor. I should have suspected something right in the beginning," said Sloan, "when Washby told me he wasn't Helen Fent's doctor. He probably took the precaution of getting her to change doctors at the very beginning of the affair so that he couldn't be charged with adultery with a patient."

Leeyes grunted. "We'll need more evidence than that . . ."

"They used to meet in the Folly," said Sloan. "We should have cottoned on to that too. Old Fitch who lived in the Keeper's Cottage down there had started to mutter about goings-on in the Folly. Nobody listened, of course. Everyone assumed he was senile and Washby got him put in a home. Easy, isn't it, when you know how?"

"I still don't see how killing Bill Fent helps."

"If he's dead," said Sloan, "nobody's to know that he isn't the father."

"Mrs. Fent . . ."

"Helen Fent isn't going to say, is she? And if she is, how does she prove it's Washby's baby and not her husband's or anyone else's, for that matter?"

"Blood groups," said Leeyes. "You've forgotten them."

"No, I haven't," said Sloan.

"They prove paternity."

"They disprove paternity," said Sloan. "That's all. Anyway, Bill Fent's blood group wasn't on record anywhere. He hadn't been in the Army and he'd never given blood as a donor—that was what that little chat over the port was in aid of—to make sure."

"They could have got it at the post mortem."

"There wasn't supposed to be a post mortem," said Sloan, the case against Dr. Washby becoming clearer every minute. "He was meant to die in his bed, with Paul Washby giving the death certificate and nobody but Paul Washby knowing it wasn't natural causes."

"Not even Mrs. Fent?" said Leeyes sharply.

"I am prepared to bet that the first time she even wondered was when she heard that there were police at the funeral. It was only after that that she was so frightened."

"Of him," said Leeyes. "Not us. Well, what went wrong with his masterly plan?"

"It was the late call for the doctor to go to Cullingoak which dished Washby's little scheme. Veronica, his wife, dialled the surgery answering machine before Washby could get to it and she gave him the message to go to Cullingoak in front of everyone, so he couldn't duck out of it. He had to go even though it meant Fent taking Berry home. The wife was another clue, by the way."

"Veronica Washby?"

"The marriage. It was a whirlwind courtship, remember. Everyone said so. I reckon as soon as Helen told him she was pregnant Washby set out covering his own position. He had a lot to lose if any of this came out, you know. Doctors do. He consolidated things very well, really," said Sloan reflectively, "except that he forgot that Marjorie Marchmont had been secretary to the late Dr. Whittaker. Someone must have reminded him."

"What about it?"

"She would have known about Bill's infertility from his medical records."

"So she had to go?"

"Washby took his car right up to the Folly this afternoon after she had been found. Much nearer than he needed to have done. I didn't think about that until later. Any traces that it left would explain any traces that he'd made there the night before. And any that she left inside the car he was busy washing off this morning with me watching him. And," added Sloan with a wry twist of his lips, "he tried to con me into thinking he was cleaning his car because it was dirty. And into thinking about the development all the time. It was nothing to do with it."

Typically the superintendent went off at a complete tangent. "The Africans believe in a matrilinear society, Sloan —that's inheriting through the female," he added gratuitously, "on the grounds that you always know who your mother is."

"It's a point," said Sloan.

"It was poured over the crémet, sir, that poison," said Crosby going over Dr. Washby's confession for the twentieth time, "and he did kill Marjorie Marchmont as well as Bill Fent but he doesn't say why."

"I didn't think he would," said Sloan.

"And now we can't ask him."

"No." The overdose that Dr. Washby had taken after shaking off Crosby had been of heroic proportions. His stunned widow had gone home to her mother.

"And Mrs. Fent doesn't seem able to help," said Crosby.

"No." Helen Fent had been found taking shelter with Cousin Hettie at Almstone. There were no men in Cousin Hettie's Eden.

"She says he must have been mad."

Sloan nodded. That was Helen Fent's story and she showed every sign of sticking to it. Of course, she might just have had that crémet instead of her husband. Say, if she'd decided to carve or Washby had been wrong about guessing where Bill Fent was sitting."

Crosby said, "Then what?"

"Then there would have been a post mortem and an inquest," said Sloan, mindful of the conscientious Dr. Baird, "but it wouldn't have got much further than an open verdict if you ask me."

"That chap Miller's no help either," went on Crosby. He was getting as bad as the superintendent for gloom. "All he knew was that his father told him that there might be something for him at Strontfield one day."

"But he didn't know why?"

Crosby shook his head. "He said to come over, keep his head down and his eye on things. Oh—and to see that old Fitch didn't want for anything."

"Old Fitch?"

"Many's the ladder up to the bedroom window he used to take away first thing in the morning for Master Hector before his father was about."

"Hector Fent knew about Bill then," decided Sloan, "but he's dead too." He pushed the case papers aside and said prophetically, "We aren't going to get anywhere here, Crosby."

"Ah, well," said the detective constable imperishably, "what's in a name?"

"You do realize, don't you, Inspector," said Mr. Puckle sternly, "that what you have just told me is pure conjecture?"

Sloan, comfortably ensconced in one of Messrs. Puckle, Puckle and Nunnery's best leather arm-chairs, nodded.

"Of course," said the solicitor, "an infant—er—*in utero* at the time of the father's death can inherit."

"We wondered."

"In fact, if the—er—circumstances which you have just—er—postulated should happen to have been the way in which the doctor attempted to solve his—er—dilemma should—er—actually have been so—which naturally I do not for one moment accept . . ."

"Naturally. But if . . ."

". . . and should the infant be male, of course . . ."

"Yes?"

". . . the only way in which he could be prevented from inheriting the Strontfield property . . ."

"Yes?"

". . . would be by a suit of bastardy brought by Quentin Fent. A successful suit, of course."

"Of course," murmured Sloan.

"And for that suit to be successful," said Mr. Puckle, giving Sloan a penetrating look, "irrebuttable evidence would be required by the Court."

"Quite," said Sloan.

"It would seem," said Puckle suavely, "that that might present difficulties."

"It might." That was an understatement if anything was.

"Where, for instance, might we look for evidence of the late Mr. William Fent's—er—incapacity?"

"Nowhere," said Sloan bluntly. "Not now. Any medical records in Dr. Washby's possession would have been amended long ago." He explained about the blood groups, too.

"Precisely. And with Mrs. Marchmont dead . . ."

"Mrs. Fent?" put forward Sloan tentatively.

"If she appeared at all," said the old solicitor dryly, "it would not be for the plaintiff."

Sloan nodded. Dr. Washby was another who had counted on Helen Fent's vested interest in silence.

"And as a married woman cannot in the nature of things have an illegitimate child . . ."

That was something else Dr. Washby had counted on.

". . . the—er—burden of proof would fall entirely on Quentin Fent." Mr. Puckle stroked his chin. "That is quite apart from the fact that under English law a person cannot be required to give evidence against themselves."

Sloan wouldn't have been surprised to know that Paul Washby had worked that out for himself too.

"And so this theory of yours," said the solicitor, "seems at first sight to be only a mere hypothesis . . ."

"It's supposition which fits the facts," said Sloan.

". . . but lacking—er—what you might call circumstantial evidence."

"Two murders," said Sloan rather shortly.

"Nevertheless," continued Mr. Puckle carefully, "should Quentin Fent be apprised of these—er—notions of yours, and were he then to ask me to give an opinion on whether a suit of bastardy would succeed, I would, subject to Counsel's opinion, advise against bringing the action on evidence of such a very—er—speculative nature."

"I see," said Sloan, matching the solicitor's detached manner.

"Theory is one thing. Proof is—er—a horse of a very different colour."

"And so say all of us," chanted Sloan under his breath. "And so say all of us."

"But if it should—er—become a matter for Mr. Quentin Fent"—Mr. Puckle had moved from stroking his chin to polishing his glasses—"he may well decide—er—in all the circumstances to—er—let sleeping dogs lie."

It was still hot.

"I hope the weather holds for them tomorrow," said Ursula Renville languidly. "I don't believe it's rained for a month."

"I know it hasn't," said Cynthia Paterson. Her self-imposed holiday was long over. It was nearly the end of September now and there was much to be done in all her Constance Parva gardens. "Everything's very dry."

"If it's not one thing it's another," remarked Ursula reaching for the tea-pot. "One thing it means is that we can still sit out of doors."

"Not for so long," said Cynthia, her experienced eye picking up signs of autumn.

"Well, there's worse things than that."

Cynthia Paterson nodded tacitly. "They've still got trouble up at the Park."

"It may be a girl."

"It won't," said Cynthia with conviction.

"You aren't a witch, you know," Ursula reminded her, "in spite of what poor Marjorie used to say."

"Poor Marjorie." Cynthia still could not think of Marjorie Marchmont without a shudder.

"Nobody seems to know why Paul killed Marjorie and Bill."

"No."

"It wasn't as if he really knew either of them well," said Ursula, voicing what everyone in Constance Parva was thinking.

"No."

"And why Bill and Marjorie," persisted Ursula. "Why not Bill and Helen Fent or Daniel and Marjorie Marchmont?"

"Don't!" pleaded Cynthia. "It wasn't 'Happy Families.'"

"It was murder," remarked Ursula astringently, "except that no one seems to know why. Or if they do," she added pointedly, "they're not saying."

"No."

"And with Paul committing suicide like he did, there won't even be a court case, so we shall never know."

"No."

Ursula looked curiously at Cynthia and then shifted her ground a little. "Do you realize if that baby of Helen's turns out to be a boy she'll have to bring him up at the Park with no money?"

"That will be a real penance, won't it?"

Ursula looked up. "Do you know, Cynthia, you said that as if you really meant it."

"I did."

"And you sounded just like your father handing out judgement."

"Did I?"

Ursula laughed uneasily. "Sentenced to twenty-one years' hard labour bringing up the next heir on next to nothing."

"It won't be much fun," agreed Cynthia.

"And if it's a girl?"

"I think," said Cynthia cautiously, "Mr. Puckle says Helen could leave the Park, take her widow's mite, and try to bring the baby up on that. So you might say it's six or two threes . . ."

"Six or two thr . . . oh, Cynthia," Ursula sounded quite exasperated, "why can't you say six of one or half a dozen of the other like everyone else."

"There'll be a little bit more than next to nothing, actually," went on Cynthia. "Now."

"Oh?"

"I hear that Peter Miller—Peter Fent, I suppose we should call him—is going to farm Strontfield as well as Fallow."

"To keep it in the family?" said Ursula dryly.

"Mr. Puckle said he thought it might be arranged, and the rent will help."

"If you ask me," said Ursula wisely, "we shall be hearing wedding bells there too. Annabel Pollock's been down for all her off-duty and he's going to St. Ninian's for Matrons' Ball."

"To keep it in the family?" echoed Cynthia meekly.

"Talking of wedding bells . . ."

"Yes?"

"Tomorrow's wedding's still on, I take it . . ."

Cynthia chuckled. "Oh, yes. Neither Jacqueline nor Quentin would be the first to back down when they heard they weren't going to get the Park if the baby was a boy. The banns had been called, you see."

"So what is going to . . ."

Cynthia actually laughed for the first time in a month. "Quentin starts in Battersby's Bearings at eight o'clock in the morning a week next Monday. In overalls."

"There's more to our Jacqueline than we gave her credit

for," said Ursula. "She'll make something of that young man yet."

"There'll be no development, anyway," said Cynthia, "unless it's a girl and Quentin inherits. And perhaps not even then." Hector Fent's son had emerged as having strong views on preserving the old pile. "Will Richard mind?"

"I don't suppose so," said Richard's wife serenely. "He's been working much too hard anyway. Besides, he's trying to get Daniel interested in golf. More tea?"

Cynthia shook her head. "I must be going."

"And I," said Ursula, "must go over and do the church flowers. Delphiniums, would you say, and a few late roses . . ."

It was still hot in the early evening when Sloan got home. He had been to the adjourned inquests on William Fent and Marjorie Marchmont and come home with his mind still on them. His wife was sitting by the open French windows knitting something white and small.

"How was I to know that Helen Fent was pregnant in time to save Marjorie Marchmont?" he demanded rhetorically.

"You weren't," said Margaret Sloan placidly.

"Hang it all, it wasn't as if she was sitting there knitting little garments . . . if he hadn't killed Mrs. Marchmont I'd never have guessed at all."

"No," agreed Margaret, "you wouldn't. So I'd better tell you now, hadn't I?"

She pushed her knitting forward a little. "The doctor says we're going to have a constable."

"What? What?" He leaped forward and out of his chair. "Are you sure?"

"No," she said calmly, "but he is."

"Constable nothing," he growled, his face suddenly suffused with pleasure. "He'll be commissioner one day or I'll want to know the reason why."

ABOUT THE AUTHOR

CATHERINE AIRD had never tried her hand at writing suspense stories before publishing *The Religious Body* —a novel which immediately established her as one of the genre's most talented writers. *A Late Phoenix, The Stately Home Murder, His Burial Too, Some Die Eloquent, Henrietta Who?, A Most Contagious Game, Slight Mourning* and *Passing Strange* have subsequently enhanced her reputation. Her ancestry is Scottish, but she now lives in a village in East Kent, near Canterbury, where she serves as an aid to her father, a doctor, and takes an interest in local affairs. Her latest book is called *Harm's Way.*